# SOCIAL STUDIES
# MAKES ME SLEEPY

## EILEEN JEDLICKA

*BOOKLOGIX*
*ALPHARETTA, GEORGIA*

Cover and Illustrations by Michele Phillips
www.michelecreates.com

BookLogix Publishing Services
Alpharetta, Georgia
**BookLogix.com**

First Print
Printed in United States

**ISBN 978-1-61005-063-0**

Visit www.eileenjedlicka.com for more information about this book.

*For all my social studies students*

# Table of Contents

Gregory

Veronica

# Prologue

She shuttered the windows tightly and doused the lamps. The little children in the rickety, one-story wooden house across the street from the docks ran to her. They grasped her long skirts tightly. The roof and windows creaked and groaned in the fierce wind coming off the harbor. Outside the shouts grew. Through cracks in the shutters she saw a crowd of men—white men—brandishing torches.

"What are these men doing?" she thought. Less than a hundred years ago this city was occupied by the British. New Yorkers died—white colonists and Negroes—to make a new country, a free country. Now, the crowds outside demonstrated against that founding principle.

It was 1843. Pro and anti-slavery factions fought bitterly even in the Empire State of New York which had outlawed slavery sixteen years earlier. Little did the warring factions know that they were setting the scene for a war, a terrible war that would almost tear the young republic apart.

That was too far into the future and unknown. For now Isabella only sought to protect her children against the forces of evil just outside the door of her little free church.

"Open up. Let us in or we'll tear your shack down stick-by-stick."

"We'll burn you down."

"Go home where you belong."

The ugly shouts rang in her ears. The children trembled. The room was dark and cold. The crowd outside was angry. Like any mob, it acted without reason.

"What could they have against me or my little ones?" Isabella said to herself clutching her children tighter and tighter. They tell me to go home. Home? I am home. My family has been here for over one hundred years. Many of the men outside just arrived months ago, some only days ago.

Why have they targeted me? Don't they realize their place in life is no better? Don't they realize the New York gentry hate them as much as they hate me? Don't they know it won't be any better for them and their children if we don't all live and work together peacefully?

Outside, the New York City watchmen couldn't control the mob. The uniformed officers watched helplessly as one man, then another, pounded the door of the little meeting house threatening to kill the woman preacher and her children.

Isabella huddled in the corner praying for deliverance. The weathered boards of the old Front Street building split. The out-of-control mob wrestled the door off its hinges and stormed into the room.

The children cried. She shivered just imagining what could happen. Could this be worse than what she lived through on the upstate New York farms? The city was supposed to be better. She had too much to live for. Too much she had to teach and preach. She couldn't leave now.

Shabbily dressed men, immigrants from all the poor countries in Europe, grasped her and pushed her down. A club grazed her head and she fell to the floor screaming for the safety of the children.

Before she swooned into a void of blackness, she looked up and saw a spirit—the spirit of Robert, her true love she was denied marrying; the spirit of her own babies who suffered so much in this prejudiced world; the spirit of what is right and just...

"Isabella, get hold of yourself," she said. "Robert isn't here. Your babies aren't here." As she lay in a puddle of her own blood, their memory comforted her. "We might finally be allowed to be together."

She looked up from the floor. She strained to see through the smoke and confusion caused by the mob storming her little meeting house. Deep back inside, flat against the wall stood Robert and her children.

"Take heart, Isabella. You have too much life to live, too much teaching ahead of you, too much truth to spread. Let us help you move on and take that sojourn where you can follow your dream."

They faded from view. The room swirled around her. The shouts of the angry crowd grew fainter. The lights dimmed. Isabella started her journey.

# Ellie

The Girl in the Chair

# 1

## Thanksgiving Dinner

At the end of fourth grade, I was Ellie, everyone's friend. I was the girl who could make you laugh. I was the girl invited to all the birthday parties. I was the girl who loved life and took everyone along for the ride.

Now, I'm Ellie, the poor crippled girl. I shouldn't use "crippled." That isn't politically correct. I'm the handicapped girl…no…the girl with a disability. People think by saying it that way, I'm not defined by my condition. What's the difference when no one will look me in the eyes anymore? I have become invisible.

A boating accident last summer robbed me of my ability to walk. I wish I'd drowned. I feel like an empty shell. My spirit is gone. My soul is gone. Where did Ellie go? Now I am nothing but a burden.

The kids at my school, Sojourner Truth Elementary, have been nice to me…too nice. They carry my books. They help me navigate the crowded halls and get around obstructions. They jump when I open my mouth.

But they don't joke with me like they used to. They don't call me stupid when I'm being stupid. They don't treat me like a regular girl. I'm different. I'm paralyzed from the waist down and probably will never walk again. I'm no longer Ellie to them. I'm the fragile girl in the wheelchair.

It was the Friday before Thanksgiving and I was

looking forward to the week's break from school, from my classmates, from my teachers, from my life. The morning crept by slowly. Social studies was particularly boring today, and I was glad to be saved by the bell.

Ms. Baumfree, the new and wonderful social studies teacher, was supposed to revolutionize the program but she didn't. At the start of the year, she gave each of us a cheap, plastic wristwatch. She insisted we wear it every day and said wearing it was part of our grade. That was exciting and mysterious but led to nothing. We just continued to read the stories of the past in our class. Why should I care about the past when I had no future?

Eric asked to push me to the cafeteria because he said he wanted to talk to me about something important. He knew that I always insisted on wheeling myself but I couldn't refuse his request today. Something in his voice moved me. Maybe I still had a little heart left because I told him that he could push me.

He whisked me to the front of the fifth grade line because now I received certain privileges, ones I would gladly give up if I could just walk again. Ms. Doris, the cafeteria lady, came out from behind the serving area and personally placed the pre-Thanksgiving luncheon in my lap. She wished me a "Happy Thanksgiving" and whispered in my ear that I still had a lot to be thankful for. I thanked her but couldn't fake a smile.

Eric and I sat at the far end of our class table to get as much privacy as possible. He smiled at me, looking into my eyes. Nothing came out of his mouth and the silence was awkward. I took a bite of my turkey just to do something. My mouth was dry and so was the turkey. I started to cough. I coughed and coughed. I was choking and couldn't catch my breath. I panicked. I grabbed my neck. My wristwatch brushed against my cheek and I heard it click. The lunch monitor ran over and then I blacked out.

When I came to, the people around me were smiling. "Just went down the wrong pipe, young lady. You'll be fine," said a very tall, black gentleman in a white coat. He placed my white linen napkin on my lap and told me to wave if I needed anything.

"Who are you? What are you doing?" I screamed.

"That's just ole Ike, our colored waiter," said the woman next to me. "Take another sip of the Polio Punch, honey. I think you were just eating this delicious Thanksgiving dinner a little too fast and it went down the wrong pipe. No need to rush now. There's plenty of food. And make sure you save room for dessert."

"My wife Bella made the best apple pies for tonight," added Ike. "As a matter of fact, she's waving at me right now to come get the pie and start serving." I looked in the direction Ike was pointing and the lady waving sure looked like Ms. Baumfree. Can't be. What's going on?

I didn't know whether I had heard anything right. I looked all around and didn't recognize anything or anybody. I was sitting at a table in a huge dining room that looked like the kind of place where you could have a wedding reception. Fresh flowers were in the center of each table. Our table had sunflowers which were my favorite. There were real linen tablecloths on the tables. Each place setting had china, fancy silverware, and crystal glasses.

The walls were a delicate tint of yellow making the room look happy. The ceiling was sky high, almost touching heaven. There were no columns or posts to block my view so I could see everything around the room.

There were hundreds of people dressed in their Sunday-best clothing. Mom made me get dressed up this morning for the last day of school so I didn't feel too out of place with all these fancy people.

I took a deep breath and rubbed my eyes but nothing changed when I opened them. I started to ask a question but was quickly shushed by the girl next to me. She said that it was almost time for Rosie to speak. I looked at my watch and it was 9:00. It was just noon in Atlanta. "How could it be 9:00? What's happening?" I cried.

"Shhhh. Rosie's getting up. Listen and be respectful."

## 2

## The Spirit of Warm Springs

A tall, handsome man at the front table slowly rose. He had difficulty getting up, even with the help of the gentleman assisting him. He leaned on the table podium that Ike brought over and steadied himself. I could see that he had heavy braces on his legs because the starched tablecloth couldn't hide that. He was sweating buckets and wiped his face before he spoke.

"Boys and girls, ladies and gentlemen, friends…it is so good to be home with all of you. There's no place like home." His smile lit up the room. The audience erupted in applause.

"Who is he?" I asked the woman next to me.

"Oh, darlin', you *were* shaken up by that coughing spell. That's Doc Roosevelt, of course. He always comes to Warm Springs to have Thanksgiving dinner with us."

"What kind of a doctor is he?" I asked.

"He's not a licensed, real doctor, silly. You know that. We just call him 'Doc' because he gives the polios really good advice and knows as much as some of the doctors about therapy and treating polio."

"His real job is actually president, honey," the man across from me said chuckling.

"President of what?" I asked.

"Stop teasin' me, sugah. Just listen now."

The clapping and cheering stopped. He started to speak again. I thought of Ms. Baumfree for a second. She welcomed me warmly at the start of school and said something to me about not letting what happened to me hold me back. She said I shouldn't expect any special treatment from her and she never gave me any. She was the only one who didn't. I remember her mentioning something about a Roosevelt in a wheelchair but I didn't pay much attention. I figured I'd better listen now.

"Members of the family of Warm Springs:

"...I don't know what the number of this party is, the eighth or ninth, or something like that, but I go back to the days when there was Fred Botts and two or three other people here for Thanksgiving, when we had our Thanksgiving party down in what we call Wreck...

"...In 1927 we had..."

"1927!" I screamed.

"Yeah, honey, you were only a little child then," whispered Ike over my shoulder.

"...80 people at the Thanksgiving party," continued Roosevelt. "In 1932 - 310 people and it was so many people that the old dining room sank three inches.

"...We made up our minds a year ago that we would never have another Thanksgiving party in that dangerous old dining room. What has happened? There are 370 people here tonight...Georgia Hall."

"So it's 1933?" I asked the girl next to me.

"Of course it is...November 30," she said in a whisper. "Now listen."

President Roosevelt continued, "...we would not any of us be here tonight unless this section of Georgia and the State of Georgia had not only welcomed us with open arms but also done everything they could to assist us in our work. For a good many years we have had the vision of Georgia Hall..."

He went on and on about the history of Warm Springs and the people who helped it grow. Most of it I understood, but I got tired of listening after a while. The yellow tint of the walls started to fade with me as I began to doze. It had been a long day...a very long day.

The applause woke me. "...You have all heard a lot about the story of Warm Springs. In those olden days, in the spring of 1926, everything depended on the way the experiment was started and, as you all know, it wasn't just a question of medical care, it isn't just a question of the exercises we all take, but it is a question of the spirit of Warm Springs..."

## 3

## Meeting Rosie

At about 10:30 President Roosevelt got in his wheelchair and wheeled himself out the dining room. The First Lady walked alongside him. They stopped at the glass, double doors leading into the dining room. He got up with some help, picked up his crutches, and balanced himself on the door as everyone exited.

President and Mrs. Roosevelt greeted the Thanks-giving Day diners. They shook hands and wished everyone a Happy Thanksgiving. I heard one of his aides say, "You really need to sit down and rest, Mr. President. You're overdoing it." President Roosevelt just smiled. I could tell from his face he was exhausted but he still smiled and said he was fine.

Each table in the dining room was dismissed in a certain order to prevent everyone from leaving at the same time. When it was our turn to go, I unlocked the brake on my wheelchair. "Don't forget your program, sugah. It's a nice memento of today and includes Doc's speech."

"Thanks," I said and stuck it in my pocket. I started to wheel myself out. I was quickly stopped by a teenage boy who grabbed the handles of my chair and said, "Don't do that or I'll get in trouble."

"What do you mean you'll get in trouble? Trouble for doing what?"

"I'm your pushboy tonight and that's what I'm supposed to do...push you."

"I can do that myself, thank you very much," I said sarcastically.

"I'm sure you can, but for right here and right now, it's my job. Just sit back and enjoy the ride." I didn't know exactly what to say or do so I just sat back.

"Robert," called one of the attendants at the door. "Bring the young lady to the front of the line with the other kids."

"Just like school," I thought, "but the difference here was that most of the kids were either in wheelchairs or on crutches, not just me." I took a deep breath and willed myself to wake up from this choking-induced coma, but I couldn't. Then and there I decided to literally and figuratively go along for the ride because I didn't have any other choice.

President Roosevelt bent as far down as he could to greet each child. He knew all of them by name and spoke to each child like a kind grandfather. He reminisced about the past with each one, finding something personal and meaningful to say to each child.

"Happy Thanksgiving, Mikey," he said to one little boy a few kids ahead of me. "And, Mikey, don't go more than 20 m.p.h. down these new halls. I saw you racing Billy outside the other day. There are patrols hiding behind the curtains in the new Georgia Hall. They give out speeding tickets."

"I'll be careful, Rosie," answered Mikey. "We don't have a lot of money and I don't think I could pay any fines," he said seriously. President Roosevelt laughed.

"Happy Thanksgiving, Elizabeth," he said to the girl in front of me. "I really enjoyed your performance at the 'Polio-Physio Follies' Tuesday night. You have a beautiful voice, Elizabeth. 'Coming 'Round the Mountain' is one of my favorite songs. One of these days you'll have to give Eleanor and me a private concert."

"Thank you, Rosie. We didn't think that you were coming to the show. I'm so glad you got to see it."

"My heart's always at Warm Springs, Elizabeth. I convinced Washington that my body had to come, too."

"I'll come and sing any time you like. Just call me."

"I will, Elizabeth. I certainly will," said President Roosevelt.

It was finally my turn to meet the President of the United States. Even though I was dreaming, I was still nervous. He took my hand and said, "What's your name, sweetheart? I haven't yet had the honor of making your acquaintance."

"My name's Ellie, President Roosevelt. I'm so happy and excited to meet you," I stammered.

"Likewise, Ellie, but please don't be so formal. All the children call me Rosie. I prefer that. You and I have a lot in common so we get to start out immediately as friends."

"Yes, Sir, President Roos....I mean Rosie. I really need a friend right now."

"So do I, Ellie. So do I." He gave me a big hug and whispered in my ear, "See you in the pools tomorrow. And...Happy Thanksgiving."

"Happy Thanksgiving to you, too." I didn't quite know how to respond to the pool thing.

# 4

## I'm Not a Polio

After I finished talking to President Roosevelt, Robert wheeled me down the long halls of the lobby and out the side door of the new Georgia Hall. It was a parade of kids of all ages, shapes, and sizes. Pushboys pushed some of the kids in the wheelchairs. Those who could walk walked. Everyone was laughing and joking and having a great time. I felt like everyone else. There was no one staring or pointing at me. I felt like I belonged. I felt like a regular kid again.

When we got out the doors, the kids parted like the Red Sea...girls to the left and boys to the right. "Where are we going, Robert?" I asked.

"You're going to your dorm to sleep. It's been a really long day."

"You have no idea, Robert," I said.

"Well, at least we can sleep later tomorrow," said one of the girls. "No school because it's Thanksgiving holiday. Mrs. Huntington said that she was glad to get a break from us."

"I never knew teachers liked breaks," said Elizabeth.

"Of course they do," said Robert. "You may not have school tomorrow but you still have pool therapy so let's get ya'll to bed."

Once we got into the girls' dorm, Mrs. Hayden, the dorm mother, met us and introduced herself to me. "Sure has been a big day for you, little lady. Coming down from Atlanta and right into a big Thanksgiving dinner all in one day. My, my! You must be tired."

"So I did come from Atlanta?"

"Of course you did, darlin'. We've been waiting for you." This was getting crazier by the minute.

Mrs. Hayden brought me down to Room 109 and introduced me to my roommate, Suzanne. "Suzanne doesn't stay with us regularly. She had surgery here a few weeks ago and is recuperating. She actually lives just a few miles down the road and comes back and forth for her therapy. She'll be here another couple of days."

"Hi," said Suzanne. "Nice to meet you."

"Hi," I answered.

"You know I'm the only patient here who doesn't have polio. I was born with club feet and Rosie said that I could get treated here along with you polios," she said.

"That's rude," I said. "Calling the poor kids here 'polios.'"

"There's nothing rude about it. That's what you're called. Nobody means nothin' bad by it."

"Well, I'm not a 'polio' because I don't have polio."

"You can deny it all you want, Ellie, but it's not going to make things go away."

"I just want this whole nightmare to go away," I said.

"So do we all."

"No. Not that nightmare. I'm not even from this time. Look at my wristwatch," I said and held out my arm. She looked at my watch and said, "Says 11:15. That's 'bout right."

## 5

## The Little White House

Mrs. Hayden helped me into a nightgown and lifted me into bed. Before she left the room, she showed me the call button if I needed anything in the middle of the night. I said "Good Night" to Suzanne and was sound asleep before my head hit the pillow. I vaguely heard her say "Sweet Dreams."

When I awoke next morning, I thought about my bed in Atlanta, but truthfully, I was glad to be waking up in Room 109. Being in Warm Springs was an adventure, a get-away from my horrible new life. I didn't feel like a freak here. I was just one of the kids.

"Let's get up, Ellie. First we'll go to the dining room for breakfast. Then you have to get to the pools for therapy," said Suzanne.

"Aren't you going to the pools with me?" I asked.

"I'll go with you," she said. "But the cuts from my surgery haven't completely healed and I can't get in the water. I'll watch you from the sides."

"Let me ask you one more thing, Suzanne. Why do the kids call President Roosevelt 'Rosie'? It was hard for me to get 'Rosie' out of my mouth. It felt disrespectful."

"That's because of me," said Suzanne smiling from ear to ear.

"What do you mean?" I asked.

"Well, the very first time I met President Roosevelt

I was about four years old. He wheeled up next to my wheelchair and took my hand. 'What's your name, little girl?' he asked.

"'Suzanne,' I answered. 'What's your name?' I asked right back.

"'President Roosevelt,' he said. 'That's a beautiful name, Suzanne. May I call you Suzie?'

"I don't know what got into me, but I said, 'You can call me Suzie if I can call you Rosie.' He laughed and said that was just fine with him. That's how me and President Roosevelt met."

"And then all the kids started calling him Rosie?"

"Yup," she said, still grinning.

There was a knock on the door. It was Mrs. Hayden. She brought Robert in to bring me down to breakfast.

"Mrs. Hayden," I said, "why does Robert have to push me around? I can do it by myself."

"I know that, dear," she said. "We need to evaluate your strength and condition. For right now, we want you to use all your energy in therapy."

I was going to argue but thought I'd just let that go for right now. "Okay, Robert, to breakfast."

We retraced our steps from last night and made our way back to the dining room in Georgia Hall. Fresh tablecloths covered the tables and everything was as it was last night. This place was like the expensive, fancy restaurants in Atlanta.

I had a huge stack of blueberry pancakes. I put pats of butter between each pancake and covered them all with real maple syrup. There were three strips of perfectly cooked bacon surrounding my pancakes. Each strip crunched when I bit into it. I washed everything down with a glass of freshly squeezed orange juice. It was the best breakfast I had ever eaten.

Suzanne had scrambled eggs, grits, and toast. Mikey was at our table and he had oatmeal with fruit. Elizabeth had waffles, sausage, and strawberries. This was not like school food. That's for sure.

"Where's Rosie?" I asked Suzanne. "Isn't he going to eat breakfast with us?"

"No," she said. "He stays and eats most of his meals at the Little White House."

"You mean he commutes from Washington?" I asked.

"No, silly. He has a house just a little ways through the woods that's his home when he's in Georgia. It sorta looks like the White House in Washington, only it's smaller. It was designed by Henry Toombs and built for Rosie. He moved into it May 1, 1932, while he was running for president. Before that he was staying in McCarthy Cottage, but that was just too small and too old," she said.

"Wait. Back up a minute," I said. "When did Rosie become president?"

"Let me give you a little history," said Suzanne.

"I hate history. It's boring," I interrupted.

"History's not boring. It's just the story of what's going on, what went on. You just asked me those questions. Do you want to know the facts or not?"

"Sorry, Suzanne. Go ahead," I said.

"Rosie first started coming to Warm Springs in 1924 after he got polio. He heard that the warm waters of the springs could cure polio so he came down to give it a try."

"But he's still in a wheelchair," I interrupted.

"It's true that he can't walk but Rosie says that the waters make him feel better. He says the warm waters boost his body up when he's in the pools and boost his spirits all the time," said Suzanne.

"He once told me that he found his soul and spirit at Warm Springs," added Elizabeth. "I'm going to write a song about that some day and sing it to him."

"Rosie was elected last November and was sworn in as president March 4," added Mikey. "The bad part about being president is that he can't visit as much as he used to. He's busy running the country."

In the middle of our conversation Robert came by. "Sorry to break this up, gang, but you have to change into your bathing suits and get to the pools for your therapy."

"It's December 1," I said. "Even though it's kinda warm today, we'll freeze out there."

"Don't worry about a thing, Ellie," Robert said. "Don't you worry about a thing."

# 6

## To the Pools

Mrs. Hayden was waiting for me when I got back to my room. She had a bathing suit on the bed and helped me get it on. It was a drab dark brown and looser than any bathing suit I had ever worn. I was used to my colorful rainbow swim team Speedo…at least when I did swim team. But I can't imagine getting into that tight suit now so this was a blessing.

I was supposed to start aquatic therapy at the Shepherd Center in Atlanta after Christmas. My parents and I had a tour of the pool and the entire facility after I got out of the hospital. The doctors and therapists said water would be very helpful in my road to recovery. I wasn't anxious to get back in water any time soon since an accident in water had caused my problem. I was angry and afraid of water.

Mrs. Hayden helped me on with my clothes and got me settled in my wheelchair. She told me that I would do just fine and gave me a kiss on my cheek. I wasn't expecting that but it sure felt good. I suddenly missed Mom very, very much. Mrs. Hayden asked me if I were ready. I nodded my head and she called Robert.

"Where exactly are we going, Robert?" I asked.

"To the pools, Ellie."

Are they in Georgia Hall?" I asked.

"No," Robert said. "They're about a mile from here.

We have to take a bus." He wheeled me to the entrance of Georgia Hall and there waiting was a new, sleek, blue bus. It was old-fashioned but very cool.

"Is that our bus, Robert?" I asked.

"Yup! That's her. You're really lucky, Ellie. That's the new Curtiss Aero Car. It's a two wheel Pullman type car attached to a Reo Coupe which is a power car. Mr. Henry L. Doherty gave it to the Foundation. You arrived when all the new changes are happening. Life is getting a lot easier here."

"We have a Foundation at my old school that provides extras for the school. I guess that's what your Foundation does, right?"

"You really are getting good at figuring everything out, Ellie.

"The polios used to ride to the pools in a very old, mud black bus that jerked and bounced everyone around. It tired the patients out before they got there. This is luxurious compared to that old thing," Robert added. "And it isn't just blue...it's called Biltmore blue. Doesn't that sound fancy!"

"Like the Biltmore House in Asheville?" I asked.

"I'm not sure," Robert said. "But it sure is a beautiful shade of blue. Makes you feel happy, doesn't it?"

The ramps under the doors were pulled out and Robert helped me get in. It was very spacious inside. He said that the aero car held twenty people or eight people and four stretchers. Only eleven were going to the pools so we had a lot of extra room.

Across the front of the bus was a divan which sat four people or could hold a stretcher. Under the seat was a compartment for crutches. I sat along the side of the bus with my back towards the window. There were two rows of four individual chairs facing one another. Suzanne and Mikey sat across from me and Elizabeth. There were more seats behind us with armrests. All the upholstering was in brown Spanish leather and the flooring was skid-proof.

Robert told me that the patients and Rosie helped the engineers design the new vehicle. There were four-wheeled hydraulics on the power car and electric brakes on the aero car. He said that made the ride very smooth.

Once everyone was on the bus, we moved away from Georgia Hall and down the long, dirt road. The windows were open and I could smell the pine trees. It felt like we were riding through a cathedral. I was excited to get going and it felt like I was on a school field trip. We were laughing and joking and got to the pools in no time. Unloading us took a while. Robert helped me out of the bus and pushed me towards the pools. A horrible feeling washed over me and that's when I panicked.

# 7

## So Much Alike

I created quite a scene outside the pools. Flashbacks of the accident flooded my brain. I sat there screaming, crying, and yelling that I would not go in the water. Robert tried to talk to me but I wouldn't listen.

The therapists came out of the water and tried to reason with me. They explained that the waters were naturally heated and about 88°. The warmth would relax my muscles and be very soothing. They said that the buoyancy was three times that of regular water so I would feel lighter and it would be easier to move. The minerals in the water did something special to the body and I would feel much better after just one session in the pool.

I wouldn't listen to any of them. I just sat in my wheelchair determined to stay dry. I knew that they wouldn't throw me in the water against my will.

After all the reasoning and arguing, there was silence. There was nothing left to say. I wiped the tears from my eyes and knew I had won the battle. No water for me. And that's when I saw Rosie.

He came towards me driving a beautiful sea green convertible sedan, smiling his big smile. Next to him sat a little black dog barking loudly. Rosie moved some gears and levers on the dashboard. The car stopped and he turned it off.

"Fala, say hello to my friend Ellie," he said. Fala barked and I half-smiled. "Fala's my Scottish terrier and we're always together."

"Nice to meet you, Fala," I managed to get out. I reached up and patted his head. Then before I knew it, Fala was in my lap licking my face.

"Fala has good taste, Ellie. Now you have another friend." I nodded. "I can see that something is bothering you. You still have tears in the corners of your eyes. What's the matter, Ellie?"

"Rosie, I just can't go into the pools. I lost my ability to walk when I was thrown out of a boat last summer. A buoy shot up in front of our boat. My dad couldn't react fast enough and hit it. The impact knocked me out of the boat. Dad quickly circled and came back to get me, but another boat was traveling too close to us. It couldn't stop and ran over me before my dad could get there. I just can't go into water ever again."

"Ellie, I wasn't always paralyzed either. I contracted polio in 1921 when I was 39. Water was involved as well."

"What happened?" I asked.

"I was yachting with my sons at our summer home on Campobello Island in New Brunswick, Canada. We had a good day sailing on the water. We also helped put out a local forest fire. It was a very busy day and I was wet and tired afterwards. When we got home, I felt as if I were coming down with a cold. I went to bed and then next morning…I couldn't move. I contracted polio."

"I'm sorry, Rosie, but I still can't go in the water."

"Ellie, listen to me," he said as he took hold of my hands. "I firmly believe the water put me where I am, and the water has to bring me back. Trust me. I believe in the powers of the special waters in Warm Springs. That's why I came down here nine years ago and that's why I will keep on coming. More than that, I believe in the spirit of Warm Springs.

"The water here helps the body, but more important, Ellie, it does something for the soul. Come with me. We'll go in the pool together."

Fala barked and licked me again. I knew I had to try. I had to try for me and I had to try for Rosie. I had to try his waters.

Rosie started up the car's engine. He told me he would park and meet me in the pools. He circled around me. Robert suggested that I watch out because Rosie wasn't known as the best driver in the world. Robert laughed.

"How does he drive when he can't use his feet?" I asked Robert.

"He has special hand controls that do the job feet normally do. He designed some of them himself. Driving is one of Rosie's favorite things in the world to do. He says that he feels like everyone else when he's behind the wheel of a car."

"Is there anything he can't do, Robert?" I asked.

"Can't walk. That's about the only thing I can think of. But that doesn't stop him from living."

# 8
## Let Your Tears Flow

Robert wheeled me from the parking lot into the pool area. There were three large pools there. One was enclosed by glass and two were outdoors. All three were connected by waterways.

"Which one am I going in, Robert?" I asked.

"We're going to the glass-enclosed pool, Ellie, because after all, it is December. We don't want you to get a chill and get sick," he said smiling. "We use that one in the cold months. Rosie's friend, Edsel Ford, gave us $25,000 to build it."

"That was nice of him. It seems that a lot of people are doing lots of things to help around here."

"People really do want to help, Ellie. President Roosevelt has a lot of friends and they want to do what they can for him and for all his friends like you."

"What are the outdoor pools used for?" I asked.

"When the weather is warmer, one is equipped with tables for various exercises. The other is used for swimming and water sports."

"What kind of sports, Robert?" I asked.

"The polios play a little bit of everything in there, but water polo is Rosie's favorite. He loves to play with the kids. That is, when they're not trying to drown him." Robert laughed.

"The glass one looks like a big greenhouse," I said.

"I guess it does," he said. "In the cold weather that one is used both for exercising and swimming. Enough talking now, Ellie. Let's get in."

Robert helped me take off my outer clothes, picked me up, and carried me into the pool. He was very strong. I felt safe in his arms even though I was still afraid. I tried to be brave. He laid me on one of the wooden tables that was bolted to the floor of the pool. The therapist was in the water waiting for me. She thanked Robert and told him she would take over. Robert gave me a wink and said he'd be waiting for me when I was done.

I really wanted Rosie but I didn't want to be any more trouble. Everyone was so nice and I decided not to complain. I wasn't a baby and thought I should stop acting like one. I closed my eyes. The warm water washed over me and felt so good. It soothed my body. I started to relax.

That's when I heard Rosie's big, booming voice. "How does the water feel, Ellie?" he said as he slowly approached me. "Didn't I tell you it was wonderful?"

When I saw him I started to cry. I tried to stop, but I couldn't. "I'm sorry, Rosie," I stammered. "I don't mean to cry, but I can't help it. I can't stop my tears."

"Let your tears flow," he said very gently. "The pool's the place for them. Letting them go will lighten your load and help you heal. Tears, minerals, friends, and warm water are a winning combination."

He gently lifted my right leg and told me to concentrate. "Concentrate on the muscles in your leg," he said. "Try to feel them with your mind."

Rosie gently moved my right leg, then my left. He moved them up and down, side to side. I relaxed and felt very light as the water lifted me and my spirits. As he was working with my legs, Rosie started softly humming. When the kids in the pool heard him they all joined in with Rosie's "Home on the Range." Everything was happening at once as if in a strange dream.

I opened my eyes and Rosie smiled at me. "You know, Ellie, I truly believe that things happen for a reason. I didn't choose to get polio but polio brought me to these kids and to you. The children have changed my life and made me a better man. Polio helped me realize the power of my soul and spirit."

I was about to answer him when I suddenly felt a twinge in my left pinkie toe. Did I really feel something or was it my fatigue and concentration playing tricks on me? Rosie looked at me and said, "Remember, Ellie, if I can be President of the United States with polio, you can do anything. Soul is who you are."

The powers of the water brought us together and for some reason I was here with President Roosevelt. "It's time, Ellie," he said. "You're ready."

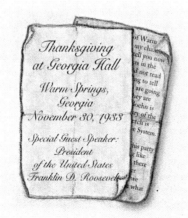

*Thanksgiving at Georgia Hall*

*Warm Springs, Georgia*

*November 30, 1933*

*Special Guest Speaker: President of the United States Franklin D. Roosevelt*

37

# Thomas

King of the Mountain

# 9

## Back in the USA

It was good to be back in the United States after spending the last three years in Germany. Dad was an Air Force pilot and had been stationed at Ramstein Air Base, the headquarters for the United States Air Forces in Europe. Our family lived on base near the town of Ramstein which is a few hundred miles southwest of Berlin, the capital.

I went to Ramstein Elementary School, a school for kids of the United States military. It was run by the Department of Defense Education Activity so it was very American. I learned German while I was there but I wasn't as fluent as the German kids. Let's just say I could get by.

We came to Atlanta because Dad retired from the Air Force and got a job as a pilot for Delta. The whole family was very excited about settling. The life of a military family was okay but the bad part was you had to move all the time. I started to feel comfortable with my new friends just about when I found out we were headed someplace else.

My parents shopped around for schools in Atlanta and settled on Sojourner Truth Elementary. They wanted a good school, of course, and it was a good school. But Mom and Dad also wanted a school that was diverse. They had been all over the world and wanted their children to continue meeting and living with all kinds of people. Sojourner Truth's student population looked like the United Nations Assembly. My parents did a good job choosing because my two sisters and I were very happy at our new school.

It was the middle of December and Mrs. O'Reilly, our homeroom teacher, took us out for recess. It was a warm afternoon for December. She said we deserved a break because we had worked so hard all week. It was always fun working in Mrs. O'Reilly's class. Actually, most of the classes were fun. But Ms. Baumfree's social studies class had been so tedious today. We memorized facts from the history of aviation. We had been doing that most of the week. I loved planes and flying but not dry info straight from the books. Ms. Baumfree said you never knew when facts would come in handy.

Before we ran off to play, we gathered as a class to sing "Happy Birthday" to Rachel who turned eleven. After the song Rachel thanked us and gave each of us a large Hershey bar as a treat. Some of the kids hung around eating theirs and talking but I ran off to play. I put my Hershey's in my jacket pocket.

The county had delivered several truckloads of pine bark that morning and it was all dumped near the playground. "Let's play King of the Mountain," I said running to get there first.

"Mrs. O'Reilly doesn't like us playing that game," said Dwayne. "She says it's dangerous."

"Don't worry. It's pine bark. We can't get hurt on that. It's soft," I said.

"Look," said Alicia. "Mrs. O'Reilly's best friend, Mrs. Emmet, just came out. They'll be talking and she won't even notice us over here."

I got to the top of the pile first and beat my chest like a gorilla. I had seen that in a documentary once and thought it was so cool. I was king for the moment.

Shandra and Ahmad tried to push me down and claim the top but I kept steady and sent them tumbling down the hill. I was easier on Shandra since she was a girl and much smaller than me. I was the true king and expertly handled every kid who tried to take my spot on the top. No one could take me down from the summit of my mountain.

I heard engines overhead and spotted a C-130J "Super" Hercules like my dad flew in Germany. It was a huge transport aircraft that was built at Lockheed-Martin in Marietta. It brought back memories of watching my dad's cargo plane take off on missions to the Middle East.

While I was temporarily distracted watching the plane overhead, Shandra slowly came up behind me. She gave me a mighty shove in the lower part of my back. She was tiny so a mighty shove from her didn't amount to much, but it was the element of surprise that caught me off balance. I toppled down the mountain of pine bark.

As I started to roll, I looked back up and saw Shandra banging her chest. I smiled and thought that was funny. I gathered steam as I rolled down the pine bark mountain. As I approached the bottom, I saw a large rock at the base. I covered my head with my hands trying to protect myself.

My wrist took the brunt of the hit. I fell on my wristwatch and heard it crack. I felt a sharp pain in my left hand. I lay there for a few seconds. When I got up I noticed blood coming from my right temple. I guess I did hit my head. I hope Mrs. O'Reilly didn't see that. She's really going to get mad.

## 10

## Sharing Chocolate

"Thomas, are you okay?" I thought I heard someone ask. I say "thought" because the question was in German. I hadn't heard anyone speak German since my family returned from Ramstein last summer, and I was rusty with the language.

I looked at the kids gathered around me. They were not my classmates. I was standing at the base of a pile of rubble, not the pine bark mountain I had just rolled down. I was listening to them jabbering in German, not English, and the plane I heard overhead was not another "Super" Hercules but an old C-54 used during World War II to carry cargo. I knew that because we had just finished studying about those planes with Ms. Baumfree.

"Where am I?" I asked. Much to my surprise, the question came out of my mouth in German. "What's going on?"

"Sit down, Thomas. You hit your head and you're a bit shaken," said a blond-haired boy with raggedy pants and a tattered jacket. His eyes were kind. He looked at me and said, "Your head's bleeding but it doesn't look too serious. Head injuries always bleed a lot."

I stared into space and figured I must be dreaming. I hit my head. I got knocked out and I was unconscious. I'll come to in a couple of minutes. Mrs. O'Reilly will hug me when she sees that I'm all right and then yell at me for playing King of the Mountain. It'll be okay.

Overhead, I heard and saw another C-54 just like the one from a few minutes ago. I followed its path and it landed a couple hundred yards away. It came in slowly and landed hard. The screech pierced my ears as it landed on steel planking. The runway was short. I was sure it was going to hit the five story apartment building at the end of the runway, but it stopped short of the building.

People were hanging out their windows waving at the plane. Only one of the people waving was black and she drew my attention. From the distance she looked like Ms. Baumfree, but that couldn't be since she didn't live in an apartment building. My eyes tricked me. I saw a sign in the distance that I could see clearly and it said "Tempelhof Central Airport."

A few more drops of blood trickled down my cheek and I reached into my jacket pocket for a tissue. As I pulled it out, the Hershey bar that I had gotten from Rachel fell out of my pocket. When I picked it up, I could feel everyone's eyes on me.

"Where did you get that?"

"I didn't see Onkel Wackelflügel come by," said a little girl.

"None of the planes yesterday or this morning wiggled their wings."

"What are you talking about?" I asked. "What's an Onkel Wackelflügel?" When I didn't get a response, I wiped away the last few drops of blood and put the tissue back in my pocket. I took the Hershey bar and opened it. I took out the chocolate and broke it up along the lines and got 12 pieces. "Twelve pieces. Twelve of us," I thought. It never occurred to me not to share.

I passed the chocolate around and no one spoke. I popped my piece in my mouth and it was gone in a second. My new friends spent the next half hour staring at their chocolate, touching the chocolate, and finally taking the smallest nibbles I had ever seen until all the chocolate was gone. I felt as if I had just witnessed some ancient ritual. When they were done, a chorus of thanks rang out.

"Danke!" (Thanks!)

"Danke schön!" (Thank you!)

"Tausend Dank!" (A thousand thanks!)

"Recht schönen Dank!" (Many thanks!)

I had never been thanked so much and so sincerely for such a small thing. "Bitte schön!" (You're welcome!) "Bitte schön!" I said twice more as a tear rolled down my cheek.

## 11

## Onkel Wackelflügel

"It really was nice of you to share your chocolate, Thomas," said one of the boys. "If I had a whole bar of my own, I don't think I would have been as generous. But I'll never have a bar because Onkel Wackelflügel never honors my requests. He never flies where I ask him to and he never drops any chocolate near me."

"No big deal. Glad you enjoyed it," I said trying to be nonchalant. "And what's your name again?" I asked.

"Tell him your name, Peter," yelled one of the boys. "And remind him that he's your best friend while you're at it."

"Shut up, Josef. He hit his head hard. Give Thomas a break. He'll come around."

"Sorry, Peter. You're right," said Josef. "And Mercedes, stop looking at me like I'm a monster. I said I was sorry."

My head stopped bleeding and I was feeling better. I decided to play along with this dream until I woke up. I didn't have much choice and it might be interesting.

C-47 Skytrains and C-54 Skymasters continued to fly overhead and land every three to five minutes according to my watch. I knew they were cargo planes and could carry tons of supplies. They were the planes that later developed into what my father flew to the Middle East. Planes were my specialty and I knew them all. I had a natural interest in aviation and Ms. Baumfree helped add a little to my wealth of information. But what were those planes transporting? It had to be an incredible amount of cargo.

My wristwatch still worked but I wasn't sure whether the time was correct. I guess that didn't matter. I looked around beyond the group and at my surroundings. I saw that the only complete building fully standing in the entire area was that apartment building at the end of the runway.

The rest of the buildings were either totally collapsed or in varying states of disrepair. There were mountains of rubble everywhere. "What happened?" I thought. "It looks like a bomb hit this place, whatever place this is."

The approaching plane was another C-54 but this one looked really different in the distance. It was shaking. No, it was wiggling. Its wings were wiggling.

"Onkel Wackelflügel!" I heard Peter scream.

"It's Onkel Wackelflügel," yelled Josef.

"I knew he would come back and wiggle those wings for us and bring us the chocolate he promised," said one of the little girls. At that point all the kids started running towards the plane. I joined them, not knowing what else to do. As we ran towards the plane, I saw the most peculiar sight in the distance—tiny parachutes descending from the plane. Armies of tiny parachutes with something hanging from them were being released from the plane.

"We're going to miss it again," yelled Peter.

"Onkel Wackelflügel's too far away and the other kids will get it before we can get there."

"Get what?" I screamed. "Get what?"

"The chocolate, you idiot! Those kids up there are going to get to the chocolate before we do."

We ran with all our might but didn't get to the parachutes fast enough. Kids lucky enough to be in the right place at the right time had already claimed the chocolate. I saw one of the boys drop something white as he ran away with his chocolate. I ran to get it. It was the parachute. I opened the little parachute and on it was written: "Please return this parachute to Tempelhof Base Operations for Operation Little Vittles."

Peter looked over to me and saw what I had. "Let's go the the airbase," he said. "Let's return the parachute now. Maybe we'll get some chocolate."

## 12

## I Just Can't Remember

We walked alone. All the other kids dispersed after they missed out on the chocolate drop, running in a million different directions looking for another chocolate plane. I was glad to be alone with Peter because I had so many questions to ask. He was supposed to be my best friend so I guessed he was the one I should go to.

"Peter," I said, "I feel fine but I can't remember anything. Something must have happened to my memory when I fell and hit my head."

"What do you mean you can't remember anything? You seem to know every plane that flies overhead."

"When were you born, Peter?"

"Same year as you, stupid," he answered. "We're both eleven."

"Please, just answer my question. When were you born?"

"July 5, 1937," he said.

I had to stop to catch my breath. If he said "1937," then that would make it 1948. 1948? How could this be 1948? It was just 2011.

"And when were you born, Thomas?" he asked mockingly.

"July 28, 19…same year as you. We're both eleven. We're in the same grade, aren't we?" I answered taking a chance.

"We used to be…when we went to school. At least you can remember that much."

"And what city is this?" I asked.

"Thomas, you're scaring me. You aren't serious, are you?"

"I'm dead serious, Peter. I don't know where I am. I don't know the date. I don't know anything about flying chocolate parachutes. Please help me remember. Please give me a quick rundown of…of everything."

Peter looked at me with the same kind eyes as when I was bleeding at the base of the rubble. He put his arm around my shoulder and said, "We've been through war together, Thomas. We can make it through this."

"War," I mumbled. "World War II?"

"See, Thomas. It's starting to come back," he said.

"Did we win or lose?" I asked.

"That's not funny, Thomas. We're speaking German, aren't we?"

"Did we win or lose?" I shouted.

"We lost, Thomas. Look around you. Does this place look like a victory?"

"What is this place, Peter? Where are we?"

"It's bombed-out West Berlin. The capital of what once was the greatest country on earth."

"Germany?" I asked.

"Of course Germany. The war's over and we're living in the aftermath of it. The Soviet Union won't let the Americans or British bring us any food or supplies. All land routes are closed. So…they started airlifting in supplies to keep us from starving."

I remembered reading about the Berlin Airlift in school. After the war, Germany was divided into four sectors. The Allies—the United States, France, Great Britain, and the Soviet Union—each patrolled one sector respectively. The Soviets occupied the eastern half while the Americans, British, and French occupied the western half.

That worked for a few years but then the Soviet Union had major disagreements with the other three countries about how to govern. The Soviets were against capitalism and democracy and believed in a communist state. They ruled their section that way. The problem was that the capital city of Berlin was totally in the Soviets' sector. The Americans, British, and French had been bringing food and supplies to the Germans in West Berlin. But then the Soviets sealed off Berlin from the Americans, British, and French. They wouldn't allow any supplies to be brought in. Trains and trucks couldn't get anything in.

The Soviets said that they would gladly feed the Germans in the Allied sections of West Berlin but they would have to adhere to Communist principles. Most Germans refused and said they would rather starve to death than give up their freedom. That's when the Allies decided to airlift food and supplies. That's what those cargo planes were doing. Now it's starting to make sense. I knew that tons of supplies were airlifted but I had no idea that planes were coming in every few minutes around the clock. I didn't know the effort was this big.

And the chocolate. I remember Ms. Baumfree reading a children's book to us called *Mercedes and the Chocolate Pilot*, but I didn't think it was real. I thought it was just a children's story—not history. Actually, it would be herstory—Mercedes' story. So some guy was dropping chocolate out of airplanes. And was that little Mercedes I met *the* Mercedes? Oh my goodness! Can this really be happening?

## 13

## Returning the Parachute

As we walked down the road, we watched more and more planes skim the rooftops of the buildings as they approached the airport. Their four propellers sliced the air on their downward descent. The planes kept coming and coming. We could see them unloading in the distance. When all the cargo was out, they got back in the air.

"Peter," I asked, "where do the planes go after they leave here?"

"They go back to Rhein-Main Air Force Base and start all over again. They reload and come back again and again and again. They're keeping us alive, Thomas. I hated the Americans during the war, but now it's different. They care about us. They really do. American and British soldiers have died delivering food to us."

"Who shot them down?"

"No one shot them down. Some of them crashed due to bad weather, fatigue, or mechanical problems. They gave their lives for us."

"Tell me about the chocolate, Peter. What was that plane doing throwing chocolate out in parachutes?"

"Hold on, Thomas. I see Brigit over there. Let's go over to her and she can tell you the whole story. She was one of the kids Onkel Wackelflügel first met."

"There's that Onkel Wackelflügel again," I thought.

We ran over to Brigit who was watching the planes unload. She was with a bunch of other kids and all of them were talking to the soldiers through the fence. I still had the parachute and thought this would be the time to return it as the note on the parachute asked. I gave it to one of the soldiers.

"Thank you, son," he said as he folded up the parachute and put it in his pocket. "I hope you enjoyed the chocolate."

"Actually, I didn't get any chocolate," I said. "I just found this parachute on the ground and returned it to you."

"But it looks like you have a smudge of chocolate in the corner of your mouth."

I licked my mouth and he was right. There was a tiny piece of chocolate stuck there. "Oh that chocolate. That's a piece from Rachel's birthday chocolate," I said. "Not from the parachute."

"Well, maybe Rachel found a parachute then. At least you got a taste. I wish I had some chocolate or gum to give you but I don't. Keep your eyes towards the sky. You never know when you'll see those parachutes coming down." The soldier gave me a pat on the head and went back in the plane. "See you later, kids," he yelled.

Brigit was about to leave when Peter called her over. "Brigit," he said, "could you tell us the story of the day you met Onkel Wackelflügel? I love that story." Peter winked at me. He really was a good friend—my best friend—at least for now.

Brigit cleared her throat. I could hear some of the other kids say, "Here she goes again." A few of them walked away mumbling that they couldn't stand to hear the story one more time. "The story gets bigger each time," said one little boy. "I'm out of here."

Brigit turned to him and stuck out her tongue. She cleared her throat again.

## 14

## Brigit's Story

"I gave Onkel Wackelflügel his name. That's what everyone calls him now and you can thank me," said Brigit. Peter let out a big sigh and Brigit silenced him with a look. There was an awkward pause and I didn't know what to do. "I'm sorry, Brigit," I said. "I apologize for Peter's rudeness. Please continue with your story. I really want to hear it."

She smiled at me and smirked at Peter. "Well, me and a bunch of other kids were standing behind a fence at the end of the Tempelhof runway one day when I first met him—Lieutenant Halvorsen, that is."

"Who's Lt. Halvorsen?"

"Lt. Gail Halvorsen is Onkel Wackelflügel," she said. "He's an American pilot. He had just landed his plane and decided to go for a little sightseeing trip while the cargo was being unloaded. He said he wanted to see more of Berlin than just Tempelhof's airport. He especially wanted to see the bunker where Hitler had spent his last days.

"Lt. Halvorsen was taking movies with his camera when he saw us at the end of the landing strip. There were about thirty of us kids and we ran up against the fence to see him. He smiled at us and said, 'Guten Tag, Wie geht's?' (Hello. How are you?)

"We greeted him in both English and German. Me and a few other kids whose English was pretty good started asking him questions in English. 'How many sacks of flour are on each aircraft?' Rolf asked him. Lt. Halvorsen came closer to the fence and told us that a C-54 could carry two hundred sacks which weighed about 20,000 pounds.

"'Don't you get tired flying back and forth all the time?' asked Alfred.

"'Yes,' said Lt. Halvorsen, 'but it's worth it to be able to help you.'

"'We have aunts, uncles, and cousins who live in East Berlin,' said Anton, 'and they tell us how things are going for them. It's not good.'

"Helena then told Lt. Halvorsen how the Soviets had taken away her grandpa's house in East Germany. 'When he complained to his friends and spoke out against the government, he was thrown in jail. And that's where he still is if he's still alive.' Helena started to cry and Lt. Halvorsen tried to hold her hand through the fence.

"That's when I said, 'After your bombers had killed some of our parents, brothers and sisters, we thought nothing could be worse. But that was before the final attack by the Soviets. They were brutal and now we won't let them put us under their form of government. I don't care if I'm hungry. My freedom means more!'

"Lt. Halvorsen listened to us with great interest. His eyes misted and he seemed to be a friend. 'My driver is calling me and I've got to go, kids,' he said finally. He walked away and then stopped. He reached in his pocket and took out something as he walked back towards us. It was two sticks of Doublemint chewing gum. He broke each stick in half and gave us the four pieces. No one shoved or pushed. I was lucky enough to get one of the pieces. We each kept the gum. We're not stupid. But we ripped the wrapper into strips and passed them around so at least everyone could breathe in the sweet, minty smell.

"Lt. Halvorsen smiled. He looked up at the C-54 soaring overhead and smiled again. He told us that if we agreed to share equally like we just did, he would drop candy and chewing gum for everyone from his plane the next day. That's when I asked him how we would know which plane he would be flying.

"He thought for a moment and said, 'When I get overhead, I'll wiggle the wings.'

"'What is viggle?' I asked.

"He held out his arms and rocked back and forth and we laughed. The next day when he flew in around noon, he wiggled the wings of his Douglas C-54. We went crazy, yelling and cheering and waving. Then we saw three candy handkerchiefs descend. We ran to get one and three of us did. But not me. Not that first day anyway.

"As the days and weeks passed, hundreds and thousands of parachutes with chocolates and chewing gum came down for us. They still do. I was lucky enough to get a parachute a couple of times. I know I'll get more. So that's why Lt. Halvorsen is called 'Onkel Wackelflügel.' (Uncle Wigglewings) I gave him that name."

"He's also called 'Der Schokoladen-flieger' (The Chocolate Pilot) and you can't take credit for that name, too," said Peter.

"I'm not," said Brigit. "And don't get so cranky just because you never got any flying chocolate."

"Is that true, Peter?" I asked. "You never got any chocolate?"

"No. I always seem to be at the wrong place at the wrong time. I've even written Onkel Wackelflügel several times and sent him drawings showing him where my apartment is. I guess he just can't find my house," Peter sighed. "At least I got a little chocolate today from you, Thomas. Thanks!"

"You're welcome, Peter. After all, you are my best friend. And thanks for the story, Brigit."

# 15

## A Package for You

After Brigit's story, Peter and I left the airfield. "Where are we going?" I asked.

"I don't know," he said. "Let's just walk."

We walked past Templehof Central Airport and carefully navigated around all the rubble. Most of the buildings were either totally or partially collapsed. I was shocked to see the devastation. Peter pointed out where Mercedes lived and he started to laugh. "What's so funny?" I asked.

"The letter she wrote. Wasn't that funny?"

"I don't know what you're talking about, Peter," I said.

"You know, the letter to Onkel Wackelflügel. The letter about the chicken hawks." He looked at me and saw that I really didn't remember the incident. "It's okay, Thomas," he said. And then he started to tell me her story.

"Mercedes' house is in the flight path of all the planes coming in, coming in every three to five minutes. It's very noisy but everyone understands and doesn't complain too much because we know that those planes are our lifeline.

"Well, Mercedes' family has chickens and her family says that their chickens think the planes coming in are chicken hawks and they're afraid of them. The chickens are so afraid, in fact, that when they see the planes coming, they run into the shelter. Some molt and haven't laid any eggs since the airlift started on June 26.

"Mercedes wrote Onkel Wackelflügel a letter with a solution to the problem. She didn't complain about the lack of eggs. She simply told him to drop chocolate when he saw the white chickens and then her family at least would have chocolate to eat."

"Did Lt. Halvorsen drop chocolate to her?" I asked.

"No, he said that he couldn't find the white chickens from the air so he mailed some chocolate to her."

"Wow. That's amazing!" I said.

"Yeah. She was the hit of the neighborhood."

"Didn't you say that you also wrote to him, Peter?"

"Many times, but so have others. Onkel Wackelflügel is busy without having to worry about me."

"Don't give up hope, Peter. Maybe you'll get a package some day."

As we walked I thought about Mercedes' story and I vaguely remembered it from that children's book. I don't know how I got here or why I'm here, but I know that now I'll look at history in a different way. It's somebody's story, some people's story to be told.

I looked at Peter and realized that he was exactly the kind of kid I would pick for a best friend, but I was born 60 years too late. At least I got to be with him today. I have no idea what comes next.

As we walked on, Peter spotted a couple of parachutes hanging from a sheared tree. "Once again, parachutes and no candy," he said. "That's been my luck all along. Here, Thomas, one for you and one for me. We'll bring 'em to Tempelhof tomorrow."

We arrived at Peter's apartment building. As we approached, his mother waved at us from the window. "Peter, Peter, it's come! It's come!"

"What, Mama? What's come?"

"A package for you, Peter! A package from Onkel Wackelflügel!"

We both smiled and ran up the steps.

# Vincent

## The Traveler

# 16

## Spring Break

Spring Break had finally arrived and I was going to New York City all by myself. Both my parents were executives for Coke in Atlanta and neither could get the week off. They decided to fly me up to New York to spend the week with my grandma. That was fine with me because my grandma was an expert at spoiling me and I figured I deserved it. I loved her very much and missed her. We always had great adventures together.

Grandma lived in Little Italy in the same tenement apartment that her mother and father moved into when they emigrated from Italy at the turn of the century. "I live on the grandest street in New York City," Grandma always says. "Why should I move?"

"Mama, you live on Grand Street," my mother would answer.

"That's what I said, Maria. That's what I said." Then everyone always laughed.

The apartment had been renovated years ago and was very cozy. It was really all that Grandma needed. She was content. She had her mother, her friends, her church, good neighbors. All that was missing was us. Hopefully, one day she will move to Atlanta and be with us full time.

My great-grandparents came through Ellis Island in 1907, the peak year of immigration. Great-grandpa died many years ago and now Great-grandma lived in an assisted living facility close to her old apartment. Grandma visited her everyday, and that's the real reason she didn't move to Atlanta with us five years ago when my parents were transferred by Coke. She said she needed to be near her mother and take care of her as long as God kept them together.

Great-grandma didn't speak much English, even after all these years in America. But I was able to talk to her because my mom and dad taught me Italian and that's actually the language we spoke at home. My family was proud of our Italian heritage and wanted to keep the language alive. All my friends thought it was pretty cool that I was bi-lingual.

Mom and Dad drove me down to Hartsfield-Jackson Atlanta International Airport on Saturday. We parked the car in short-term parking and walked over to the terminal. It was always crowded at Atlanta's airport but it was extra crowded today because of the Spring Break exodus.

The Delta check-in line was long, but most of the people were in a good mood since they were going on vacation. I had one suitcase which I checked and one carry-on bag that had all my important stuff: iPod, Game Boy, cell phone, magazines, a book, and one pair of underwear. The underwear was Mom's idea in case my suitcase got rerouted to Alaska or somewhere. She said you always needed clean underwear. It was easier to pack it than argue with her.

After I checked-in and my bag was put on the conveyor belt, the desk attendant leaned over towards me. "Here's a pair of flight wings for you, honey. It will make your trip more fun." She pinned them to my shirt and I thanked her, but when we turned the corner I took them off and gave 'em to a little kid I saw. I was too old for that junior pilot stuff. I had traveled alone before and felt confident without the wings.

We proceeded to security. The line snaked around the queue and into the food court. It moved slowly but we had given ourselves plenty of time so we weren't worried. Mom and Dad had gotten special permission to go with me all the way to the gate since I was traveling as an unaccompanied minor. I was glad for their company.

"Vinnie, you know that we really are going to miss you while you're up in New York."

"I know, Dad, but you'll have me back before you know it."

My mom got all teary-eyed and didn't seem to know what to say. "Your eye looks good, Vincent. That sty is down to almost nothing, but remember to put the cream on it every night until the sty's completely gone."

"I will, Mom. I promise. The cream's in my backpack in a quart-size baggie so security doesn't give me a hard time."

"I guess you're all grown up, Vincent. You've thought of everything."

I looked at her and knew what she needed to hear. "Yeah, Mom, but I'll always be your little boy." She smiled and hugged me.

After about 45 minutes we reached the head of the line. I was in front of my parents and finally ready to go through the scanner. "Let me get you a bin," Dad said.

"I can do it, Dad. Thanks anyway." I picked up one of the gray plastic bins and put my backpack in it. I took off my sneakers, my jacket, and my Yankees baseball cap and put everything in there as well. Seconds before going through the body scanner, I realized I still had my school wristwatch on so I took it off quickly and just stuck it in my shirt pocket. I didn't think it would cause much of a problem since it was plastic and a piece of junk anyway. It couldn't activate anything. The only reason I took it with me was because Ms. Baumfree made me promise I would when she heard I was going to New York City.

I had my boarding pass in my hand and I waited for the security agent to wave me forward. I glanced over the agent's head and noticed a lady experiencing a pat-down by one of the female security personnel. The lady sure looked like Ms. Baumfree but I knew she couldn't be. Ms. Baumfree said she was staying in Atlanta for Spring Break.

"Okay, son. Your turn," the agent finally said. I proceeded through the scanning device. As I stepped through, sparks shot out of my shirt pocket. I could smell plastic burning and heard a faint click. Smoke flooded the area and I started to shake and sweat. The last thing I remember was the agent running towards me and my mom and dad screaming from behind. I collapsed before anyone could catch me.

## 17

## An Unaccompanied Minor

I opened my eyes and saw a crowd of people around me staring. I felt very self-conscious and tried to stand up as fast as I could, but I got dizzy. I wobbled and fell back down.

"Don't get up, son. Just lay there a few minutes until you feel better. You just passed out. We want Doc Meyers to take a look at you, but I don't think it's anything serious. I'm sure it was just all the excitement of finally seeing the Statue of Liberty and the long boat ride."

"Statue of Liberty? Long boat ride? I hadn't done that with Grandma yet," I mumbled. And this guy wasn't the security agent who just waved me through. This man was wearing a heavy serge jacket, starched collar, bowtie, and a boxy hat. He looked like the conductors on the Long Island Railroad. That was odd.

"Where are my parents?" I asked.

"You speak great English," said the man.

"Of course I speak great English. I'm American, ain't I?"

"Well, not quite yet, but hopefully, very soon."

I didn't know what he was talking about. "Where are my parents?" I asked again, this time more upset.

"We looked at the papers you had in your hand and the ship's manifest pinned to your shirt. You're unaccompanied and meeting your grandma in New York City at the dock."

"Dock? I am an unaccompanied minor but my parents should still be with me here," I said choking back tears.

"They are, son. In spirit," he answered trying to calm me down. "I'm sure your grandma will be at the Kissing Post and meet you after you're processed."

"What are you talking about? Let me have my boarding ticket back. I want to see something." He gave me the papers but it wasn't the boarding pass I had at Hartsfield-Jackson. It was an official-looking document. I scanned it but didn't understand what I was looking at. "What is this thing?" I asked.

"It's your paperwork and everything seems to be in order. You're Vincent Accardi and you sailed steerage from Palermo, Italy, on the *SS Madonna*. You're eleven years old and you're traveling by yourself. Your grandmother will be meeting you once you're processed and have passed all the tests. You look healthy so I'm sure you'll pass with no problem."

"What tests? What are you talking about?"

"Let's just get you up now and I'll take you to Doc Meyers. I'll watch out for you, Vincent. Don't worry. We Italians always stick together."

"That's what my family always says," I answered.

"They're right, Vincent. They're right."

When I got up, the crowd moved to give me room. The cargo shorts and the Birkenstocks and the North Face jackets everyone was wearing at the airport in

Atlanta were gone. The people staring at me were dressed like the third-class passengers on the *Titanic* movie: long skirts, shawls, knickers, hats. I panicked. Tears flowed down my face and I started to shake.

"Calm down, Vincent. Everything will be fine," the agent said with kindness in his voice. "Where are your shoes? Did they come off in all the excitement?"

"No, they're in the bin over there," I answered, trying to compose myself. "I put them in the gray bin with my backpack, my jacket, and my Yankees cap before I went through the scanner."

"So you're a Yankee already! That's a very positive attitude, Vincent," he said.

"Actually I'm a Braves fan but I wear my Yankees cap when I come to New York. I want to fit in and not get harrassed."

"Vincent, I can tell that you'll soon fit in and you are very brave. But as far as the bins, we don't have any bins, and I don't know what you mean by a scanner," he said. "Don't worry though. We have some extra shoes and hats with the lost and misplaced clothing. I'm sure we can find something suitable in your size."

I closed my eyes and rubbed them really hard. I hoped that would wake me up, but when I opened them I was still shoeless and hatless with the *Titanic* people. The agent who was helping me was still by my side. I saw that his nametag said: "Ellis Island: Agent Marco Colombo."

None of this was making any sense. I was really sweating now. I reached in my pocket to get the tissues that Mom had insisted I take. They weren't there but I found my wristwatch. I smiled and was consoled that I wasn't totally losing my mind. I did put my watch in my pocket before I went through the scanner. I did! The watch was melted a bit but still ticking. I did smell burning plastic. I'm not going crazy.

I calmed down and tried to think rationally for a minute. A million things went through my mind. What was happening to me? And then it hit me! My parents were giving me one of those super expensive, real-life simulation experiences for a Spring Break present. They felt guilty that they couldn't take time off from work. They're trying to make up for it with this gift. I read about real-life simulations and once saw a documentary about it. I'm on a big set and all these people are actors and actresses in period costumes. That's it.

But those kinds of things cost thousands and thousands of dollars. I *am* worth it and my parents can afford it and I am their only child. No, can't be. That would be ridiculous. I rubbed my eyes again and nothing changed. Well, I'm just going to play along. I don't have any other choice.

# 18

## Your First Lesson

Agent Colombo was very kind. He made me feel a little more secure. He told me to sit down on a bench in the corner of the Great Hall while he went to get some shoes and a hat for me. He measured my feet using the length of my identification papers. He asked if he could keep them for a while and use them to find the right size shoes. I said, "Sure."

That's when he said, "Vincent, I am going to teach you your first lesson. Never give up your papers or anything else important to a stranger. Don't let them walk away with your valuable stuff—whether papers, clothing, or money. You can't trust just anyone."

"But you're not a stranger, Mr. Colombo. You've helped me."

"I know, Vincent, but I want you to learn to be careful. Now I'll be right back. Wait here."

"No, Mr. Colombo. I'm coming with you. You have my papers."

"That was just an example, Vincent. I really will be right back with shoes and a hat. I work here and I'm responsible."

"Sorry, Mr. Colombo, but I'm coming with you."

"You certainly learn fast, my boy. That's very good. Come on with me," he said with a smile.

We walked into the Baggage Room of the Main Hall Building. Mr. Colombo and I weaved our way through the crowds to a back room. He came out with a box of shoes. I rummaged through it until I found a pair of dark brown lace-ups that fit. They were old and they were smelly, but they fit.

Mr. Colombo next brought over a hat rack which was in the corner of the room. On it were derbies, straw hats, top hats, fedoras, and poorboy caps. I noticed the boys my age I had passed were wearing those poorboy caps so I picked out one of those. I thought it would help me fit in and not feel so conspicuous. Mom said never to put on other people's hats because you could get lice. Under the circumstances, I didn't think she would mind so I put on my poorboy cap.

After I got my hat and shoes, Mr. Colombo said we had to go up to the second floor for the medical inspection. "Walk straight and strong, Vincent," he said. "The testing has begun. The inspectors are watching everyone as they ascend the stairs. It's the first part of the test. They're watching to see how fit the immigrants are."

I straightened my back and tried to look strong and confident as I walked up the stairs with Mr. Colombo. The long lines of people slowly made their way up the stairs. I felt guilty walking right up and not standing on line but Mr. Colombo told me to follow him. I tried to ignore all the nasty stares.

"How long will those people have to wait?" I asked him.

"Once you get there, the questioning only takes a few minutes but the whole inspection process averages about five hours."

"Wow! Standing on line and waiting for five hours," I said.

"Well, that really isn't that much time when you

think about the end result. If you pass all the tests and questioning, you get to pass through the gateway to the American dream."

"What happens if you don't?" I asked.

"If you don't what?" Mr. Colombo said.

"If you don't pass."

"Don't worry," he said as he patted me on the head. "You'll be just fine. You're smart. You're healthy. Your grandma is waiting for you. You'll be in New York in no time—a real Yankee who speaks great English!"

"I couldn't have made it without you, Mr. Colombo," I said.

We were finally in the Great Hall of the Registry Room. There were a lot of doctors and nurses there, but Mr. Colombo only wanted me to see Doc Meyers. Doc was his friend and Mr. Colombo said he was the best doctor at Ellis Island. We looked around a while and then Mr. Colombo spotted him examining a man with the longest beard I had ever seen in my life. "I think that guy's smuggling in something in his beard," Mr. Colombo chuckled. I laughed, too.

Mr. Colombo grabbed my hand and held it. We slowly walked towards Doc. "Are you ready, Vincent?" he said kindly.

"I am, Mr. Colombo, and thanks for everything. Grazie!" (Thank you!)

"Prego, mio figlio. Prego." (You're welcome, my son. You're welcome.) He bent down on one knee and looked me straight in the eye. And then…all the color drained from his face.

# 19

## Eye Trouble

"What's the matter, Mr. Colombo? You look like you've seen a ghost."

"Vincent, what do you have on your right eye?"

"Nothing. What do you mean?"

"Your right eye is a little red and you have a tiny lump on your lower eyelid."

"Oh, that. It's nothing. It's just a sty and I have...I mean I had cream for it. It'll go away in a few days. I get them a lot."

Mr. Colombo was still on one knee when Doc Meyers came over. He introduced me to Doc. The doctor looked at me and shook my hand. Then he got a look on his face similar to Mr. Colombo's. The doctor took something out of his pocket. Mr. Colombo said, "Don't Nathan. Give the boy a chance. He's a good kid." I didn't know what was going on.

"You know we can't, Marco," he said to Mr. Colombo. "I'm sure he's a good kid, but he could infect everyone." He took the chalk he had in his hand and wrote "E" on the shoulder part of my shirt. Then he waved to one of the nurses and she came over. They talked for a few seconds. She took my hand and started to walk off with me.

"Wait a minute," said Agent Colombo. He gave me a hug and pinned all my papers to my shirt. "Where is she taking me, Mr. Colombo? I didn't have my physical yet." He started to say something but she whisked me away so fast I couldn't hear what he was saying.

We walked briskly to the stairs and started the long trip down. I saw that some people were going off to the right and some to the left. Those on the right side were smiling, laughing, and talking in a million different languages. Those going off to the left were either quiet or crying. I prayed that she take me down the stairs and to the right, but I was sure that wasn't what was going to happen.

When we turned left at the bottom of the stairs, I felt sick. "Where are you taking me?" I cried.

"Calm down, Vincent. We're just going to the hospital for some testing."

"Mr. Colombo said that I looked like a strong boy and wouldn't have any trouble passing medical," I said.

"You do look strong, Vincent. The problem is your eye."

"It's just a sty. It'll be gone in a couple of days."

"Let's just hope that you're not gone in a couple of days," she answered. That silenced me. I realized that everyone wasn't as kind as Mr. Colombo. I was scared.

We left the building through the back exit. She said that we needed to steer clear of as many people as possible since I might be contagious. Today was the busiest day yet at Ellis Island and thousands of immigrants were coming through. "What day is it?" I asked.

"Friday," she answered.

"No, I mean date and year."

"April 17, 1907," she said. Then I heard her mumble, "Seems like he has a lot more wrong with him than just his eyes." I didn't ask her any more questions because I feared the answers.

## 20

## Chalked

When we got to the hospital, the nurse told me to sit on the bench in the front lobby and not to move. I was the only one there. I took consolation in the possibility that I was in my parents' simulation gift. But this was too real. This was too scary. They would never put me through something so terrifying. Too many people were involved. There were too many buildings. This wasn't a set. This was real. I started to pray.

After a few minutes, a different nurse came out. She had a mask on. Every part of her was covered up except for her eyes. I couldn't see her mouth but it seemed as if her eyes were smiling. "Hello, Vincent," she said. "I'm Nurse McFee and I'm going to take you inside. You'll have to wait a little while until you're called in for your examination." When she heard my moan she told me that everything was going to be all right. I didn't believe her.

Nurse McFee took me into a very large waiting room that was filled with people. The room divided into sections. She brought me near the window where there were two other kids. I looked at them. They looked at me. None of us said anything.

While I was sitting there, I glanced at them and noticed that each had an "E" on their clothes like me. I took a quick look and saw that the boy had a black eye. I couldn't see anything wrong with the girl. "So we're the eye people," I said. "The 'E' must mean eye trouble. I wish I had my sty cream."

I looked around at the different groups of people in the room. I noticed that each group wore a different letter written in chalk on their clothing. Some had "H." Some had "L." Others had "S," or "K," or "Pg." There were only women in the "Pg" group. Each of them was pregnant so I figured the "Pg" meant "pregnant" and they were going to have a baby. I didn't know why that should be a problem. I would think they were healthy if they were having a baby. Everyone looked as scared as me.

The two kids in my group started talking to one another in Italian. The boy asked the girl if she were scared. She said that she was and started to cry. He put his arm around her and told her that everything was going to be all right. That's what everyone around here was saying but I didn't believe it.

"I can understand Italian," I said to them. "I know what you said."

"You don't look Italian," said the boy.

"And you're not dressed Italian," said the girl.

"You're not dressed like anything," said the boy. "You look weird."

"Well, I'm not weird and I am Italian. I'm Italian-American."

"You wish," said the boy. "They're never going to let you into America."

"Yes, they will."

"Shut up. I told you you're not getting into America," he yelled. When he grabbed me, the girl pulled him off and said, "Antonio, calm down. This kid is going to give you another black eye. He looks tough. Just leave him alone. Please."

They sat down together. Antonio again put his arm around the little girl. They looked a little alike so I thought they must be related. "Are you brother and sister?" I asked. Antonio growled, but the little girl said, "Yes, we are."

"You're lucky to have one another," I said. "I feel so alone and scared."

"We'll be your friends. My name's Rosa," said the girl, "and this is my brother, Antonio. He always protects me."

"Where are your parents?" I asked.

"We got separated at the stairs. The doctors put this 'E' on me because of my crossed eyes. My brother got the 'E' because of his black eye which he got onboard the *Madonna*. They took us here to be checked."

"My papers said I was on that ship. How did you get the black eye?" I asked Antonio.

"Some jerk was making fun of Rosa's eyes so I hit him. No one makes fun of my sister or any member of my family."

"I see he hit you back," I said.

"Yeah, but he looks much worse than me. They need to check us out to make sure that we're not contagious. Our parents passed all the exams. They'll be waiting for us after we're checked out."

"What if you don't pass?" I asked. When I said that, Antonio jumped up and Rosa once again pulled him back down. "I wonder if they have a letter to put on him for anger management?" I thought.

Rosa, Antonio, and I sat there for about an hour. Then another nurse came for us. "Hello. I'm Nurse Jawicki," she said. We walked down a long corridor and went into an examining room. She told us to sit in the back. There were two other groups in this room. One was marked with a "C" and one was marked with a "Ct."

"Don't go over to anyone in those other groups," the nurse said.

# 21

## The "Buttonhook Man"

Nurse Jawicki left for a couple of minutes and then returned. "Okay, tough guy. You first." I thought she was talking to me, but she gently took Antonio's hand. He pulled his hand out of hers and said, "I'm not going anywhere without my sister."

Then it was Rosa who put her arm around Antonio. "Go with the nurse, Antonio," she said very calmly. "Vincent will watch over me. Everything will be all right."

"Go ahead, Antonio. I'll take care of Rosa," I said. "After all, we Italians stick together. We're family." He smiled at me. I didn't think he knew how to smile.

I asked Rosa if I could put my arm around her. She said I could and cuddled close to me. When I held her, I realized how small and fragile she was. That's when I admired Antonio and knew I would have taken a black eye to protect her any day. She seemed so brave when she spoke to her brother, but she was shaking now.

"Rosa," I said, "Antonio will pass the exam. Don't worry. He just has a black eye. There's nothing contagious about a black eye. I'm sure they just want to see if he has any damage to the nerves in his eye or any broken blood vessels."

"I know, Vincent. I'm not worried about Antonio passing the eye exam. I'm worried about me. His black eye will go away but my crooked eyes won't. They won't want me in America with these eyes. I look so funny."

"First of all, Rosa, you are beautiful and so are your eyes. They cross a little but that can be fixed. They have doctors in America who can fix that very easily. My uncle is an ophthalmologist in New York. I'll give you his address. He'll help you. And you're not contagious so you'll get into America with Antonio and your family. Believe me, Rosa. I know what I'm saying."

Nurse Jawicki came back and called for Rosa. "Did my brother pass? Is he okay?" Rosa asked.

"We're not allowed to give out that information," she said. And then she winked at Rosa and smiled. Rosa waved at me. I was so relieved.

And now I was alone. Alone on this bench. Alone at Ellis Island. Alone 104 years before I was born. Uncle Mark wouldn't be in New York when Rosa got there. Uncle Mark hasn't even been born. And how could Grandma be there? Grandma hasn't been born. Maybe Great-grandma will be there. But I won't even know what she looks like.

Nurse Jawicki came and got me. "It's your turn to see the doctor, Vincent. Let's go."

"Did Rosa make it? Please tell me."

Nurse Jawicki looked at me, took a minute, and said, "Rosa and Antonio are going down to meet their parents. They're both fine, Vincent." I breathed a sigh of relief.

"Thanks for telling me, Nurse Jawicki. I really appreciate it."

"I know, Vincent. I know."

When I got in the examining room, Nurse Jawicki introduced me to Dr. Frank. "Hello Doctor," I said. "My eye's really fine. It's just a little sty that's actually going away."

"Let me be the judge of that, Vincent. Just relax. I'm going to take a look at your eyes."

Dr. Frank grabbed an instrument from the table. He held it by the handle. It had a hook at the end of it. He brought it up to my eye. I was pulling away. "Hold still, Vincent. If you move, I could poke you and cause some damage." He then used it to turn my eyelid inside out. The pain was intense and I screamed.

"Your left eye looks good, Vincent."

"There's nothing wrong with my left eye. It's the right one that has the sty," I said quite angrily.

"When you're sent here, Vincent, we have to check both eyes." That's when I started to feel sick because I realized that he was going to do the same thing to my right eye with that hook.

"Are you ready?" he asked.

"No, but go ahead anyway." I braced myself and dug my fingernails into my hand. I thought of Rosa going through this moments before. I couldn't be a coward. "Ouch!" I yelled. I figured even brave guys yell.

Dr. Frank smiled at me and said that I only had a sty which would go away in a couple of days. I knew that from the start but decided to keep my mouth shut. He told me to apply warm compresses morning and night once I got settled in New York. "Settled in New York?" I said. "You mean I passed?"

"You passed, Vincent. Your eyes are fine. I took a quick survey of the rest of you and you're very healthy."

"Can I ask you a question, Doctor?" I said.

"Sure, Vincent. I think I owe you that much."

"The other people in the room had either a 'C' or 'Ct' on them. What do those letters stand for?"

"You are an inquisitive boy, aren't you?"

"I'd like to learn as much as I can from this experience," I replied.

"Those marked with a 'C' are suspected of having conjunctivitis. If they do, they will be treated until it clears and then released. The 'Ct' is much more serious. Those marked with a 'Ct' are suspected of having trachoma. That's what I tested you for when I flipped your eyelids. I didn't think you had it, but since you were chalked for eye problems, I had to test you."

"What's trachoma?" I asked.

"Trachoma is a contagious disease that could lead to blindness. We can't take the risk of people with trachoma coming into America."

"You mean those people have to go home?"

"Unfortunately, yes, Vincent. They are sent back to the country from which they came. Most people who return to their countries have to go back because of trachoma."

"What about their families? What if their families

passed all the exams and they didn't? Do they all go back? Or do the families stay in America and just send home the person with trachoma?"

"That's a very hard decision that they have to make," he said. "Those people don't call this place 'Ellis Island.' They call it 'Heartbreak Island.'" I was so glad that Rosa and Antonio's family didn't have to make that decision.

Doctor Frank opened the door and called for a nurse. I was sorry to see that it wasn't Nurse Jawicki. I had really liked her. "Vincent, this is Nurse Colombo. She's going to take you to finish the rest of your Ellis Island processing," he said.

I thanked Doctor Frank for everything. He shook my hand and wiped the 'E' off my shirt. I was really glad to see that go. "You're going to be fine, Vincent. You'll be in New York before you know it."

I walked out with Nurse Colombo. We walked up those same stairs that I had walked down a little while ago. "These stairs have a special nickname," she said. "They're called the 'Stairs of Separation.' A lot of families part ways here for health and other reasons. It can be very sad."

"I'm glad that Rosa and Antonio got reunited with their family."

"Always thinking about others, Vincent. You're a good boy. I think there will be a happy ending for you, too."

I told her that I had met a really nice man when I first arrived and his name was Colombo. "My husband," she said. "And yes, he is a very nice man. We're going to him right now." That was the best news I could have heard.

## 22

## The Golden Door

I ran to Agent Colombo and I wrapped my arms around him. "I was so scared," I sobbed. "I've never been so scared. I've never felt so alone in my whole life." He held me for a few seconds as his wife looked on.

"Vincent, everything is going to be fine," he said. "Let's go to the Registry Room where I'll process you myself."

"Can you do that?" I asked.

"Of course I can, Vincent. That's my job." He asked for my manifest and I smiled. "You're not going anywhere with it, are you?"

"No, Vincent. I'm not. I see you haven't forgotten what I've told you. That's good." I gave him my manifest. He verified all the information on the sheet.

"Everything looks in order," he said. "Let me pin this back on you so your papers don't get lost or stolen."

"Is that it?" I asked.

"That's it. Welcome to America."

"What happens now?" I asked.

"Let's get you something to eat before you leave,"

he said. "You must be starving."

"Come to think of it, I am. I was too scared to be hungry before."

"Let's go to the dining room. I haven't eaten today either so I'll join you."

We walked to the dining room in silence. I hadn't realized how exhausted I was from the day's ordeal. I couldn't imagine going through all this and getting shipped back to Palermo. Or to Atlanta. Or to wherever it is that I'm from.

Agent Colombo came over to our table with two trays. The plates were filled with beef stew and potatoes and rye bread. On my tray there were also crackers and milk. "Dig in, Vincent," he said. "The food's very good."

The food was actually delicious. Real home cooking like my grandma makes… And then I got scared again. "What happens if Grandma isn't there to meet me, Agent Colombo?"

"Don't worry, Vincent. She'll be at the Kissing Post."

"What's the Kissing Post?" I asked.

"It's where all the happy family reunions take place."

"But what if she's not there. What if I can't recognize her? What if I'm left all by myself?"

"Vincent. If she's not there—but I know she will be—Mrs. Colombo and I will adopt you. You'll join the four kids we have waiting for us on Grand Street. We'll be one big, happy Italian-American family." He laughed and hugged me.

"You live on Grand Street?" I asked, not believing what I'd just heard.

"Yes, I do, Vincent. And everyone knows it's the grandest street in New York City!"

# Gregory

The Dreamer

## 23

## **Daydreaming**

Social studies always made me sleepy. Today was no exception. I looked out the window, daydreaming as usual. The window I sat near caught the intense glare of the morning sun. The sunlight was strong. The warmth comforted me as Ms. Baumfree read aloud about the Underground Railroad and escaping slavery. Her voice was soothing and had a hypnotic effect on me. I tried to picture myself on a train with Harriett Tubman but sleep was overtaking me.

My eyelids got heavier and heavier with each word. My head started to bob up and down. I tried with all my might to stay awake. I could hear the kids around me whispering and giggling. "It's Gregory's naptime. It's Gregory's naptime." I tried to hold my head up with my hand. My wristwatch dug deep into my cheek and it hurt. I readjusted my head so the watch wouldn't pinch so much. I heard a click from the watch as I dozed off.

All of a sudden the window pane shimmered. I saw those strange patterns I see when my flat-screen TV turns on. I knew I must still be daydreaming because the window started to look like my TV. I stared real hard and saw a crazed teenager outside. He was running towards the school shouting and waving a sign. The sign said "It's time!" Time for what? What was he yelling about?

The clock on the classroom wall read 11:00, but the last time I looked at my watch it was only 8:00. I glanced at my wristwatch—11:00. Could I have been sleeping for three hours?

I studied my classmates. I must still be dreaming. I wasn't in my classroom. Ms. Baumfree was gone. The teacher in front of the room sorta looked like her, but the hair and the clothes were definitely not hers. And these children certainly weren't my classmates. Everybody in the room was black. A few minutes ago I was one of eight African-Americans in my fifth grade social studies class. The rest of the kids came in different colors.

Before I had time to question the situation further, several of the kids stood, went over to the windows, and opened them up. To my surprise, they climbed out of the windows and shimmied down the drainpipe to the ground below.

"Come on," shouted one of the girls. "You said you were gonna go. You promised."

"This is our moment. This is our chance to do something," yelled another. "Get up. Let's go after our freedom."

I was usually bored during social studies class but these kids were taking it to the next level. I was bold enough to sneak a nap but would never climb out a window to escape. I figured I could endure anything for forty-five minutes.

I looked up at the Ms. Baumfree look-alike and saw that she was facing the blackboard and not looking at the class. I also could see that she had a smile on her face. This was the weirdest daydream I had ever had.

The kids remaining in the room had a thirty-second debate among themselves. "This is D-Day and we have to go downtown. Our parents couldn't protest with Dr. King for our civil rights so we have to do it. Let's go with them."

"My Momma said she would kill me if I was part of this thing," said a bespectacled, timid boy.

"Well, either your Momma will kill you now or being a Negro in Birmingham will kill you later."

"Negro? Birmingham?" I screamed.

"Yeah, on to Birmingham, Negro!" the rest of the class yelled and dragged me out the window with them.

## 24

## On to Birmingham

"Did you listen to The Playboy this morning?"

"Do him, Jerome. You imitate The Playboy better than anyone."

"Yeah, Jerome. Do him," everyone started chanting. "Do him."

A little kid about seven years old picked up a stick and spoke into it deeply. "Good Goobly Woobly. Good Morning, children. This is Shelley 'The Playboy' Stewart. Don't forget, kids, there's going to be a party in the park and don't forget your toothbrushes 'cause luncheon will be served."

"What is he doing? What is he talking about?" I asked a sweet-looking girl who I hoped wouldn't snap at me and make me feel more stupid than I already did.

"You must be shell-shocked over the excitement, fool. Jerome's doin' Shelley 'The Playboy' Stewart, the DJ at WENN. Ya know, 'The Mouth of the South.' He loves us kids and he's been talkin' code all week to get us ready for today."

"You mean the picnic in the park?" I asked. She looked at me as if I were from another planet. "Yeah. The picnic in Kelly Ingram Park."

I figured I'd better not ask any more questions and just move along with the crowd. The best I could do was listen and try to figure out what was going on. This seemed to be the only way to survive until I woke up from my daydream which was quickly turning into a nightmare.

"Dr. King didn't know that we kids were going to do it at first," said the girl who had been sitting next to me in class.

"Do what?" I asked. I just couldn't keep my big mouth shut.

"March, stupid. When Rev. James Bevel told Dr. King he would help him fill the jails, he didn't realize he meant with kids."

"Jail!" I screamed. "We're going to jail?"

Then everyone started chanting, "Jail! Jail! Jail! We're going to jail!"

One girl reminded the crowd. "Remember what Rev. Shuttlesworth said. This is supposed to be a silent demonstration. No songs, no slogans, no replies to obscenities."

At that point, I nearly wet my pants. I didn't know The Playboy. I didn't know Rev. James Bevel. I didn't know Rev. Shuttlesworth. I didn't even know what an obscenity was. I had heard of Dr. King but he was dead. Maybe I'm dead too, and by jail they mean I'm headed for somewhere other than heaven.

I looked over my shoulder. Kids were coming out the front door, out of the windows, out the basement. On the front steps, the teachers and principal just moved aside because there was nothing they could do to stop them. It was a human stampede.

More kids joined us as we marched down the street. They came from all directions. First it was just the kids from our school. Then hundreds more appeared. Then thousands. They were coming from all over the city and even from outside the city. I had never seen so many kids in all my life...and they were all black. Everyone was black. Where were all the white people?

I noticed the cars on the street as we weaved our way around them: an old powder blue Ford Fairlane, a classic red Pontiac GTO, a vintage lime green Chevrolet Impala, a Ford Cortina—whatever that was. These cars were out of a car museum. The parking lot of my real school only housed SUVs, trucks, and sedans in subdued colors. I felt like Dorothy in the *Wizard of Oz*. "Toto, I've a feeling we're not in Kansas anymore."

I reached into my pocket and took out a box of Orbit gum. I had sneaked it into school that morning. I popped a piece in my mouth and watched the kid next to me stare. "Want one?" I said.

"What's that?" he asked.

"Gum," I answered.

"That sure is funny lookin' gum. Don't you have any Black Jack?"

"First of all, the gum doesn't come in black. And second of all, my name's not Jack. It's Gregory."

He just looked at me. I knew that once again we were talking a different language. He took a piece. "Thanks," he said. "My name's Eddie."

He unwrapped the gum and gently put it in his mouth. "Pretty good," he said. "But I do like the licorice taste of Black Jack better." After a few seconds, I figured that Black Jack must be a type of gum. I was learning quickly.

"I noticed you carefully folded the wrapper, Eddie, and put it in your pocket. Is littering a major crime in Birmingham?" I asked trying to be funny.

"I don't know," he said. "I don't really care anything about littering. I'm saving this wrapper for my gum wrapper chain. It's almost six feet long."

I didn't want to ask another stupid question. I figured that a gum wrapper chain was a chain made from gum wrappers. That was good enough for now.

After walking a bit further, I said, "Eddie, where are we going?"

"To the Sixteenth Street Baptist Church. Come on, boy. Get it together."

"I don't have anything to get together," I mumbled.

One of the girls from my class started softly singing "Our Day Will Come" as we got closer to the church. "Never heard that," I said. "Is it a Negro spiritual?" trying to be friendly. Again I got the "Are you stupid?" look.

"No, it's not a Negro spiritual. It's Ruby & the Romantics. It's the #1 hit on the Billboard Hit Parade. The Playboy plays it all the time."

"Give me a little credit. Aren't we all hoping our day will come?" I mustered up the nerve to ask her.

"Yeah, you're right," said Eddie. "That's a good one, Gregory. Don't listen to her and her uppity attitude."

I moved along with the crowd and we soon reached the Sixteenth Street Baptist Church. We poured into the church and filled every inch of space available. Those who didn't fit in the church stayed outside in the back.

I just listened and took it all in. It was the biggest pep rally I had ever seen. Rev. Bevel was clapping his hands and jumping up and down. His face glistened from the sweat that ran from his skullcap to his brow. His clothes were drenched. The church was sweltering but the heat seemed to energize Rev. Bevel.

"Anybody here from Parker High School?" he yelled.

"We're here, Reverend," a large group in the back screamed. "We're here."

He ran towards them shouting, "Alleluia! Alleluia!" Then he called out, "Do we have Lincoln Elementary?"

About two hundred kids got up waving and screaming. "We're with you. We're with you all the way."

"Praise Jesus!" Bevel said. "And Western-Olin High, are you here?"

"Here we are, Reverend. Here we are," they screamed.

When he called Washington Elementary, the kids from my new school got up. "Get up, Gregory. Stand up," they yelled. When I stood up with Washington Elementary, when I stood up with my new classmates, I was prouder than I had ever been in my life. We made more noise than any other school. The energy and excitement were contagious and my fears were going away.

When the kids started singing "We Shall Overcome," I joined in. I knew that song from a social studies video on the Civil Rights Movement.

## 25

## Our Parents Can't Fix This

The singing ended. An eerie silence enveloped the church. Maybe I can take a few minutes to sort this out while it's quiet.

I know my name is Gregory Simmons. I know that a short while ago I was sitting in my social studies class at Sojourner Truth Elementary in Atlanta, Georgia. I looked at my wristwatch and it was 8:00. Ms. Baumfree was reading aloud from the textbook. I was staring out the window daydreaming as usual. Her melodic voice always had that effect on me. I was leaning on my wrist and now here I am in the Sixteenth Street Baptist Church in Birmingham, Alabama.

My thinking time didn't last very long. Rev. Bevel was waiting for Dr. King to arrive. It was past noon. When Dr. King didn't come, Rev. Bevel opened the front doors of the Sixteenth Street Baptist Church. He let fifty kids go out. They went down the stairs and walked towards the park. I figured they were going to that picnic everyone was talking about. And then from the windows, I saw the white people.

The police—the white police—had their men and equipment laid out like a battlefield. They gathered up those fifty children and put them in police paddy wagons driven by white drivers. The children were being arrested. "Why are they being arrested?" I screamed.

"Because they're parading without a permit."

"They're just walking to the park. The First Amendment says that they can do that," I said.

"Not in Birmingham. A couple of weeks ago city officials made any racial demonstrations illegal. They got scared when some Negroes in Birmingham met about equal rights and staged a small demonstration.

"The park's the green buffer between Negro Birmingham and white downtown. As long as we stay in the Negro section it's okay. But we're threatening white Birmingham now."

"Why can't they go through the park and downtown?" I asked again.

"Are you some kind of idiot? I already told you. They're Negroes. You're a Negro. We can't demonstrate for equal rights, especially near the white section of Birmingham."

"Well, Atlanta's pretty close to here and I can go anywhere I want to go. I can do anything I want to do there."

"No you can't, you liar. My cousin lives in Atlanta. He says it's not as bad as Birmingham, but he still has to drink at the colored water fountains and go to the colored bathrooms. He can't do whatever he wants to and neither can you."

"You're crazy. What are you living in the Dark Ages or something?"

"That's kinda funny. Dark Ages? Yeah, these are the dark ages of May 2, 1963."

"1963?" I screamed. Then I started to shake uncontrollably. One of the high school football players came over to me and put his arm around me. He was about 300 pounds but had a touch as gentle as a butterfly. "What's your name, son?"

"Gregory," I said.

"Listen, Gregory. We're only kids but we have to do this. We're used to our parents fixin' everything for us but they can't fix prejudice and segregation. Our parents can't demonstrate because they'll lose their jobs if they march. They're afraid. Their bosses are white and many would fire them if they thought they were protesting. They'd make their lives worse than they already are."

"But all white people aren't like that. My best friend's white. Daniel and his family would never treat anybody badly. The color of someone's skin doesn't matter to them," I said.

"That's a beautiful thought, Gregory, but I think you're dreaming."

"Maybe so," I said.

"There are good white people in Birmingham, too, but they're afraid to speak up. They're afraid of the white power structure in charge. The adults are afraid to act.

"Remember the meeting with Dr. King, Gregory? When he asked who was with him and who would fill up the jails, only us kids stood up. As much as he was afraid to use us, he listened to Rev. Bevel. He's letting us do it.

"And the movie that Rev. Bevel showed us about the Negroes in Nashville trying to peacefully eat at a white lunch counter? What happened? They got their heads bashed in. They just wanted to eat and they got their heads bashed in. Do you want that to happen to you here in Birmingham? We'll demonstrate peacefully, let the world see, and we'll be all right.

"Now be brave, Gregory, because God is on our side."

"I hope God's black," I said.

Everyone around me laughed and I felt a little better. Rev. Bevel released the kids from the church fifty at a time. As they went out the front door of Sixteenth Street Baptist, more kids came into the church through the back door.

After about an hour, we didn't see the paddy wagons anymore. Jefferson County school buses replaced them. This was quite an education!

Rev. Bevel told my group to get up. I walked down the stairs with my new classmates. I should have been scared, but I wasn't. Something about being part of this huge group gave me courage. I knew something special was happening and for some reason, I was a part of it. I didn't want to wake up from my dream anymore. I was a part of Dr. King and his dream now.

The police escorted us onto the next school bus. We were happy and we were singing. Little Jerome took a sign out from his shirt and stuck it against the window. Only one word was written...in crayon. "Freedom."

The police arrested 973 kids that day for parading without a permit. There were so many kids in jail that the schools closed. I shall never forget what happened on May 2, 1963, in the city of Birmingham.

# 26

## Gathered in Prayer

Dr. King paced his room at the Gaston Motel. He received reports of the day's happenings and worry lines creased his smooth brow. The children's fate troubled him. He second-guessed himself and the wisdom of listening to Bevel. Should children be used to expose the gross injustices in Birmingham to the world? Dr. King shook his head and sat in the rickety chair in his room. He closed his eyes in prayer.

Birmingham was nicknamed "Bombingham" because of all the unsolved bombings that had taken place in the city. The city was vicious and violent. Eugene "Bull" Connor, the Commissioner of Public Safety, made life unbearable for the Negroes. The Civil Rights Movement's organizers wanted him out of office. They wanted his white army tank that he drove around the city to go with him. The leaders of the movement figured they needed to demonstrate in the middle of the day rather than be murdered one by one in the middle of the night.

That night Dr. King met with parents of the jailed children in Sixteenth Street Baptist Church.

"Dr. King, my child's in jail."

"Dr. King, my baby's arrested. What'm I gonna do?"

"Dr. King, I'm so scared."

Dr. King spoke to the parents. "Don't worry about your children. They're going to be all right. Don't hold them back if they want to go to jail for they are doing a job for all of America and all of mankind."

He gathered them in prayer. They knelt, heads bowed. They held hands and asked the Almighty for the strength, the courage, and the perseverance to continue in this battle, this fight for equality.

A radio played in the background. The Playboy's voice pierced the soulful quiet of the impromptu prayer meeting. "Listen, brothers and sisters," he said. "If today was D-Day, tomorrow will be double D-Day."

The parents prayed even harder.

# 27

## Interrogations

When we got to jail, we were processed. There was a lot of waiting around because there were almost a thousand kids. The police fingerprinted us and took our mug shots. I was number 30667 and proud of it.

Some of the older girls combed their hair and put on make-up because they wanted to look good for their picture. Their purses overflowed with all sorts of things: hair curlers, perfume, clean underwear, and…toothbrushes and toothpaste. So I guess The Playboy wasn't kidding. They were ready, but this wasn't exactly the picnic I had in mind. No chicken, no potato salad, no lemonade. All we got to eat that day was one bologna sandwich on dry bread. It didn't matter because I wasn't even hungry.

During the course of the afternoon and into the evening, the police took us out one by one to interrogate us. Bull Connor gave that order. When the two detectives took me to the interrogation room, some of my old fears returned.

The room was empty except for a dirty table with one chair. I sat down. It was dark. A single bulb hung from the ceiling right over my head. The larger detective started the questioning.

He leaned up to my face and shouted, "Why did you march?" I could smell the garlic from his lunch and it made me feel queasy. I didn't answer him.

"Why did you march?" asked the other. I could see that his bald head was shiny. I figured that maybe I wasn't the only one who was scared. I said nothing. "Who told you to march?" he persisted.

"Were you forced to march?" added garlic-breath. He unwrapped a piece of gum and put it in his mouth. I was grateful for that since it would mask his smell. He asked me if I wanted a slice. I was shocked. He handed me a piece of Black Jack. I put it in my pocket for later. I thanked him but told him that I still wasn't going to answer any of his questions.

Even if I knew the answers, I wouldn't have given them any information. I was scared but could feel the football player's powerful arm around my shoulder. The memory gave me courage. One kid being interrogated by two grown men wasn't fair. None of this was fair.

After an hour of questioning, I returned to my cell. It felt so good to be back with my cellmates. The day's events energized us. We weren't tired. We sang all night long. We had to be quiet during the protest. Rev. Shuttlesworth said so. But he also said we could sing our hearts out in jail, and we did.

*Ain't scared of your jail, 'cause I want my freedom,*
*I want my freedom,*
*I want my freedom.*

*Ain't scared of your jail, 'cause I want my freedom,*
*I want my freedom now!*

It was a long night and I was glad when morning came. I figured we'd be out of jail before breakfast, but I was wrong. We stayed there that second day. We had company, lots of company. Another 1,922 were arrested Day 2. It was getting very, very crowded.

Some of the kids coming in were bloodied. Most of them were wet. But they were all glad to be with us. They were happy to be in jail. Their stories of the protest made our experiences seem tame.

## 28

## Open the Hydrants

The kids newly arrested said word of what had happened to us yesterday spread quickly throughout Birmingham. We were on the news last night. The Playboy shouted our praises over the airwaves. We were famous.

Today more than 3,000 spectators lined the streets by the church to watch the second day of the protest. No one could have imagined what did happen.

The children once again assembled at Sixteenth Street Baptist Church. "Are you ready for today?" shouted Rev. Bevel.

"Yes. We're ready for anything," answered the children.

"The police may spit on you today. Are you ready?"

"Yes!"

"The police may hit you with their night sticks. Are you ready?"

"We're ready."

"There may even be dogs."

"We're ready."

"They will take you to jail."

"That's why we're here," shouted the children. "We want to go to jail."

"But remember, children. Don't fight back. Don't curse back. Don't spit back. This is a peaceful demonstration. God is on our side."

"Praise Jesus!" they yelled. The children again sang "We Shall Overcome."

Thousands of Birmingham's children streamed into the park. And they kept on coming. Nothing could stop them.

Bull Connor thought he could. He stood defiantly in front of the swelling crowd of children. "Go home. There's nothing you can do."

He waded into the crowd shoving and pushing but none of the children would yield. They just swarmed around him and passed him by. Connor broke free, shoving a little girl. She fell down. He stepped right over her and faced his police.

Connor's face was bright red. Beads of sweat dripped down his forehead. He grasped the tie of his police chief. As he screamed into his face, his jowls shook. "I want you to restore order. Now! Tell the fire department to affix hoses to the hydrants. Blast these kids to Kingdom Come. Do it now!"

The police chief motioned to the fire chief. He made a sign with his hands to attach the fire hoses to the hydrants and turn them on. The fire chief and his battalion commanders looked troubled. Sure, spray a burning building to put out a fire and save lives. But use the powerful hoses on little children? What was Connor thinking?

The chief gave the order to open the hydrants halfway—just enough pressure to scatter the children but not enough to hurt them. His firemen screwed the hoses to the hydrants and halfheartedly aimed them at the little boys and girls. Despite Connor's order, they were careful to aim the powerful streams of water at the children's legs.

It worked. Children ran this way and that, trying to escape the blasts of the fire hoses. "Okay, boys. That's enough. The kids are gone."

The fire chief grabbed the hydrant wrench out of the hands of one of his men and turned off the water. When he turned around, he saw about ten children still standing in the park singing and shouting one word over and over again. "Freedom."

Bull Connor was beside himself. Shouting to no one in particular, the hate-filled Commissioner of Public Safety yelled out, "Ain't no one gonna do that to me!"

All reason left his mind. This was no longer a battle between the laws of the city—however wrong—and the demonstrating children. This was personal. This was between Bull Connor and a bunch of kids who made him look like a fool. And the "Bull" was going to get even.

"Hit 'em again. Open the hydrants all the way. Let's see if they still can stand there and defy me."

"The increased pressure is too much. Hundreds of pounds of water pressure can break bones," said one the firefighters to the chief. "We can't do that to kids."

"If you want this job, you'll do it," the chief screamed.

The new stream was so powerful that it took four firemen to hold one hose. One of the blasts hit a tree and the bark of the tree went flying off from the pressure of the water. Another blast loosened some of the bricks from the wall of a building.

"The water stung so bad," said one of the kids. "I went flying in the air and had no control."

A little girl added, "When the spray hit me, I slid across the entire block from one corner to the next." She showed us her bruised and bloodied arms and legs.

The firemen sprayed the children relentlessly. The crowd had seen enough. The first bottle thrown from the crowd landed at the feet of Bull Connor. He knew it wouldn't be the last. The crowd threw bottles, rocks, and garbage at the police and firefighters. Bull Connor got in his white army tank. That's when he called out the dogs.

A pack of German shepherds bared their teeth and snarled at the crowd of children in the park. A frightened little boy ran from one dog right into another dog. The vicious animal bit the child in the neck. Blood spurted from his throat. The boy screamed, cried, and grabbed at his neck before he fainted. An ambulance took him to the hospital.

The battle at Kelly Ingram Park was a living nightmare.

## 29

## A Troubled President

Front-page headlines and photos in newspapers nationwide spread the news of the vicious Birmingham attack on helpless children. America saw babies chased by dogs, run down with blasts of water from fire hoses, and battered by upraised police batons. The scenes horrified mothers and fathers sitting around their kitchen tables.

President Kennedy sat in the Oval Office with his head in his hands. The photos sickened him. He stared at the shot of the little boy attacked by the German shepherd. Then he looked across his desk at a photo of his little son, John-John. How could this happen in America?

The president called Dr. King and told him to stop the movement. Dr. King told President Kennedy that it was out of his hands. He couldn't stop the children even if he wanted to. Some children got out of jail and then they went right back. They wanted to be in jail because they wanted their freedom.

Demonstrations continued. Some kids went downtown in their bathing suits ready for the spraying they knew they were going to get. The police arrested 4,163 the third day.

Children filled the jails. Children filled the jail yard. Eight hundred children sat in the hog pens at the fairgrounds. There was no more room in Birmingham to hold the protesting children.

There was no end to the number of children converging on Birmingham. By Tuesday, May 7, the city faced a state of total collapse. Thousands of students stampeded downtown in a victory lap. Water and dogs weren't working any longer. The police were helpless. White Birmingham panicked.

City officials agreed to meet with Dr. King and the movement's leaders. After 72 hours of negotiations, Dr. King appeared on TV. "I am very happy to be able to announce that we have come today to the climax of the long struggle for justice, freedom, and human dignity in the city of Birmingham."

The Negro children of Birmingham defeated the city's racist system. Facing total instability and chaos, the white citizens of Birmingham agreed to integrate. State officials removed Bull Connor after seven terms in office.

"Good Goobly Woobly. This is Shelley 'The Playboy' Stewart. Well, folks. It's official. Mr. Eugene 'Bull' Connor is out of a job. Bull Connor was beat by the young people of the city of Birmingham."

For some reason, I was a part of the Children's March that wakened the nation to the horrors of prejudice. White Birmingham tried to preserve their segregated way of life any way they could. But they never saw the secret weapon coming. They never thought it could be children.

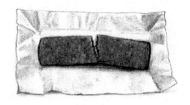

# Veronica

## The Poetess

# 30

## Released from Prison

Ms. Baumfree dismissed our class. We left the social studies classroom, and I felt as if I were released from prison. It wasn't really her fault but I blamed her. She used primary source documents whenever she could. I found them interesting. I was one of the few students who did. Looking at birth certificates and prison records and period photos made history come alive. I know Ms. Baumfree would never intentionally hurt anyone's feelings, but today hurt. It hurt terribly.

We were studying World War II and I felt like the enemy. The word "Japs" in some of the headlines made me cringe even though it was presented in the historical context of the war. And the editorial cartoons were too painful to look at. Many of them portrayed the Japanese with over-sized teeth, thick glasses, and exaggerated slanty eyes.

I stopped in the bathroom before going to English because I needed to cry. I needed to cry and I needed to hide. I wanted to stay there for the rest of the day but I'm so straight, I couldn't skip class. I got scared when the bell rang and I knew I was late. I splashed water on my face and ran into English.

Mrs. Arthur was about to say something to me but then stopped. I sat down and tried to cover my face. "I think we'll do something a little different today," she said as she glanced at me. "I think we should take advantage of the beautiful day and go outside."

"Yeah! Recess!" said Manuel.

"I didn't say we were having recess," Mrs. Arthur said. "I said we were going outside."

"Sunday's Mother's Day," said Cecilia, "and we really need to finish our poetry books to give to our moms as a present."

"That's exactly what we're going to do," said Mrs. Arthur. "We're just going to do it outside. Let me go over the format of the last poem we have for our book. Then we'll go outside for inspiration."

"If we finish fast, can we play?" asked Devon.

"No," said Mrs. Arthur. "There won't be time. We have to write our haiku, finish all our illustrations, and wrap up the book as a present. The forty-five minutes will barely be enough time. If you don't finish, you'll have to take the paper and ribbon and do the wrapping at home."

"Great," I thought. "Haiku. Just what I needed. More attention to being Japanese. Why can't I just fade away right now?"

"Haiku is a form of poetry from the Japanese culture," said Mrs. Arthur smiling at me. "'Haiku' means 'playful verse.' It is non-rhymed so there will be no rhyming in this poem. Haiku was written in a single vertical line by the Japanese but in English we use three horizontal lines of five syllables, seven syllables, and five syllables. Chose a season. Use imagery to create your haiku."

"Last year Mrs. Meyers taught us that haiku needs to be about nature," said Chris.

"Yes, focus on nature but make it seasonal. Chose a season. Explore the nature of that season. Use all your senses. Let's do a couple together to show you."

140

Mrs. Arthur wrote two poems with the help of the class so we could get the idea. I tuned out because since I'm Japanese, I should be the expert. Right? Today was a totally racial profiling day as far as I was concerned. I just wanted to get away.

When the class finished the two poems, Mrs. Arthur told us to take everything we needed with us: paper, pencil, poetry book, colored pencils. She then took out a big box and gave each of us either a sheet or towel or blanket. "What are these for?" I asked.

"When you go outside, I want you to look around you for inspiration. Then, if you like, spread your sheet or towel or blanket on the ground. Lay on it and look up. Observe from another perspective. Examine the clouds, the trees, the birds flying in the air. Be careful not to look directly in the sun."

"Cool!" said Mark.

Mrs. Arthur gave me a king-size sheet with bright flowers on it. I thanked her and got on line, grateful that she didn't say anything more to me.

When we went outside I walked off by myself. I wanted to be alone with my thoughts. I spread the sheet under a flowering dogwood tree. It was large and I had a difficult time getting all the corners down. I lay on the sheet's field of purple flowers and stared at the leaves overhead. I could barely see the blue sky and wispy clouds through its branches. The sun warmed my skin. I tucked my hands under my head and shifted a bit. My wristwatch pinched my neck. I heard a click. I suddenly felt very sleepy and thought that a little power nap wouldn't hurt.

## 31

## My Dogwood Tree

When I woke up from my nap I had the perfect haiku in my mind. It formed while I slept. I sat up, jotted it down quickly, and then read it aloud.

*Umbrella dogwood*

*Filtering all life's evils*

*Growls at my enemies*

It didn't rhyme. That was good. It was about spring and nature. Check. It didn't strictly follow the 5-7-5 syllable pattern, but I didn't care. Mrs. Arthur said that writing rules were meant to be broken when what we had to say was important. I felt as if this tree were my protector so the poem was going to stay 5-7-6.

With my haiku finished, I closed my eyes and laid down to take one last look at my dogwood. It was gone. I was laying under an apple tree. There were hundreds and hundreds of small apples overhead—no dogwood flowers. Could I have rolled while I was napping or walked in my sleep? I sat up and saw that I was in the middle of a bunch of apple trees. No dogwoods in sight.

I started to panic but tried to calm myself down. "Let's just lay back down, Veronica," I said, "and my tree'll be back. Some kind of poetic imagery mix-up just happened. I was too into that poem. My brain temporarily got squeezed and rerouted."

I kept my eyes closed while I counted to one hundred, figuring that that should do it. When I opened my eyes, the apples were still staring at me. They were laughing at me. "Okay. I'm still sleeping, and I'm dreaming. It's just a dream."

A girl appeared out of nowhere and waved. "Come on, Veronica, let's get back to class before Mrs. Matsui gets mad. She said we only had 20 minutes to write our poem and we've been out here longer than that."

"Who is Mrs. Matsui?" I thought. "Mrs. Arthur gave us 45 minutes," I yelled back. "We still have time."

I gathered up my stuff and threw everything in the flowered sheet. I didn't recognize where I was so I kept my eye on the girl and followed her. We ran through what seemed to be an apple orchard. There were hundreds of apple trees all around. Pear trees soon replaced the apple trees. Once again, hundreds of pear trees in an orchard. This certainly was beautiful, but I knew that my school grounds did not have trees like these. Where was I?

The girl slowed down. "Come on, Veronica, hurry up!" she yelled.

I continued to run as fast as I could. When I reached her, I didn't recognize her at all. "That's why she didn't say 'Mrs. Arthur,'" I said. "She's not in my class. I guess another class was writing poetry outside just like us. But why does she know my name?"

"Come on, Veronica. Let's go," she said again. "We're going to be late."

"Who are you? How do you know my name?" I asked.

"Stop fooling around, Veronica. If we're late one more time, Mrs. Matsui's going to tell our parents. She warned us last time. And our parents have enough trouble. They don't need to worry about us being disobedient."

"Last time when? What kind of trouble? Being disobedient?" I said.

"Stop echoing me. You know I hate that game."

I didn't have any more time to think so I stuck to my "I'm still sleeping theory." This was one of those lucid dreams I'd read about. I'm sleeping and dreaming and I know that I'm in a dream. I had no control over what was going on so I figured I'd follow… "What's your name?"

"Miko, wise guy!"

I figured I'd follow Miko.

# 32

## Relocation Camp

I stood at the door staring like a deer-in-the-headlights. "What's wrong with you?" Miko said as she took my hand and pulled me towards her. "You're scaring me, Veronica," she said. "Stop acting so weird. Snap out of it." I was scaring me, too.

We entered a building that looked like an army barracks. There were about thirty children inside sitting on chairs at two large tables. They were all Japanese. The room was dimly lighted with no windows to add any natural light. The walls were painted a drab green. Children's work hung on them. In front of the room stood a woman by a blackboard. She held a piece of chalk in her hand. "I'm glad you decided to join us, Miko and Veronica," she said. "Sit down please."

"Sorry, Mrs. Matsui," said Miko. "We got lost in our poetry." There was silence and everyone was staring at me. Miko gave me a shove and mouthed "Sorry" and pointed at Mrs. Matsui.

"Sorry, Mrs. Matsui," I said.

"Apologies accepted," she said.

We sat down and Mrs. Matsui spoke. She also was Japanese. "I know that you have been very busy with your poetry. Tomorrow we will have our sharing. Tonight at home I want you to pick out your favorite poem of all those you've written. I want you to memorize it for recitation in front of the class. It may be any style, any length, any subject. Practice tonight so you recite it with feeling. I am looking forward to our poetry sharing very much." Then she dismissed us.

The students got up and filed out very orderly. I got up, too, even though I didn't know where to go. "Veronica," said Mrs. Matsui, "where are you going?"

"Home," I said. I figuered Miko would direct me like she'd been doing all afternoon.

"Did you forget?" she asked.

Forget what, Mrs. Matsui?" I said.

"You're staying with me tonight. Your parents are staying with your brother overnight at the hospital. Remember?"

"Is he all right?" I asked. I didn't know where I was or what was going on, but I did have a little brother.

"He's fine," she answered. "Just a broken leg from his fall out of the apple tree. They set his leg but the break was a little complicated. They wanted to observe him overnight and your parents didn't want to leave him alone. He was very scared. They knew that I'd take good care of you.

"Just sit down and I'll be ready to leave in a few minutes."

I sat down. As I waited I looked around the room and noticed how bare it was. No posters, few books, no desks. This certainly wasn't Sojourner Truth Elementary in Atlanta. I looked at the blackboard. We didn't even have blackboards any more. Each classroom in my old school was equipped with white boards and a SmartBoard.

148

Poetry filled the blackboard. The poems were quite good and very deep. There was nothing fun or playful or light about any of them. I did laugh, however, when I noticed that there wasn't one haiku. Everyone was Japanese here and not one haiku.

My eyes went to the top of the blackboard and there in beautiful cursive was written "May 18, 1943." That's when I screamed.

## 33

## Our Nightmare

Mrs. Matsui ran over and put her arms around me. "What's the matter, Veronica? Tell me what's the matter."

"I'm in a terrible nightmare, Mrs. Matsui, and I can't wake myself up," I said.

"We're all in that same nightmare, Veronica. At least we're together and we have one another."

"You don't understand. I don't belong here. I'm not from here. I'm not from this time."

"Veronica, none of us are from here. Being brought to the Manzanar Relocation Camp was not our choice. Your family and my family and even Miko's family were very happy living in Little Tokyo in downtown Los Angeles. We had a good life—a good life until Pearl Harbor."

"So what are we doing here?" I asked.

"The United States government is afraid of us, Veronica. They fear all Japanese. They think our fisherman are spying on the Navy ships. They think our farmers want to poison the food and water supply."

"Why isn't the government afraid of the Germans and the Italians? We're at war with them also. Why aren't they here?"

"The government is afraid of the Germans and Italians in America, Veronica, but the Germans and Italians can blend into the general population. They can't be rounded-up as easily. Our looks are distinctive. We can't mix in the way they do.

"Even though we are Nisei second generation and American citizens, the government doesn't trust us. They think we are all spies and will send important information to the Japanese government.

"President Roosevelt established the War Relocation Authority on March 18, 1942, which set up relocation camps for all people of Japanese heritage living on the West Coast. There are ten camps. They're all here in the far West except for the two in Arkansas."

"You mean we're in a concentration camp and we're going to be killed. I'm not Jewish, are you, Mrs. Matsui?"

"Hold on, Veronica. First and foremost, we are not going to be killed. How did you ever get that in your mind? Second of all, I'm not Jewish either. I don't know what that has to do with anything. And lastly, I don't even know what you mean by concentration camps. I've never heard about them."

"Sorry, Mrs. Matsui. I'm just not making any sense." I then realized that if we were really in 1943, the world hadn't yet found out about the concentration camps. And if I had paid more attention to my history in Ms. Baumfree's class, I might have known about these Japanese relocation camps.

"Mrs. Matsui, where exactly are we? Where is Manzanar?"

"All of a sudden you're the geography student," she said with a smile. "We're in the Owens Valley in

Manzanar, California. We're about 225 miles northeast of our home."

"Los Angeles?" I asked.

"Of course, Veronica. Los Angeles. The Owens Valley had once been an apple and pear region but it was abandoned because of a water shortage. 'Manzanar' actually is a Spanish word that means 'apple orchard.'"

"But I was writing my poetry under an apple tree, Mrs. Matsui. There are hundreds of apple and pear trees out there. And my brother fell out of an apple tree."

"The orchards are thriving thanks to our men, Veronica. When we first came to Manzanar, there wasn't much growing out there. The camp residents built an irrigation system and pruned the trees. In no time, the trees decided they wanted to be back with us. By the fall of 1942, we had a rich harvest." She smiled.

"The Manzanar farmers cultivated fifteen hundred acres despite the harsh conditions and barren land. The turnips and corn and all the other vegetables are used in the camp kitchen. Our men raised chickens, pigs, and cattle and so we also have meat. We're luckier than some of the other camps.

"When we first got the notice that we had to leave our homes, the government told us to prepare for a 'pioneer life.' I had no idea that they really meant it."

"Like Laura Ingalls Wilder?" I said.

"Not exactly, Veronica. Let's go now. It's time to go home."

## 34

## Girls Can Play Baseball

Miko was sitting on the steps outside when we opened the door. "Can Veronica and I play a little, Mrs. Matsui? Please. I'll have her home in time for dinner. I promise." Mrs. Matsui looked at me and smiled. "Go ahead, girls. Have some fun, but don't forget about your poetry."

"We won't," the both of us said in unison.

Miko took my hand and we walked arm in arm. I guess we must have been really good friends so I asked her. "Miko, how do you feel about being here in Manzanar?"

"This 'wartime community,' as the government calls us, is a prison without cells. I hate it here. I hate every single minute of every single day. Every night I pray that my day was just a horrible dream and that I will wake up in Los Angeles. But I don't."

"There's a lot that's nice around here. The orchards are beautiful. Mrs. Matsui is more caring than most teachers I've had. We have each other."

"But we lost our freedom. We're American citizens and we've lost our freedom. My parents used to have a grocery store in Los Angeles. After the bombing of Pearl Harbor, they had a big sign made and hung it in front of their store. It said: 'I AM AN AMERICAN.'"

"Most of our customers stopped coming to the store. Soon it was only the Japanese who came in and bought anything. And then we got the order to leave.

My father hastily sold the store and all its contents for 5% of what it was worth. One of the Caucasians bought it. Father lost almost everything he had worked so hard for his whole life."

"I'm so sorry, Miko. I didn't know."

"Not many know the whole story." Miko got teary-eyed and I hugged her. "And my grandma... The government confiscated Grandma's knitting book. The idiots thought that 'knit one, purl one' was some kind of code. Can you believe that? Grandma loved that book and they took it." Miko broke down in sobs and I held her. I held her long and hard.

When I felt Miko's breathing start to return to normal, I said, "Miko, let's go. Let's get out of here and have some fun."

We walked a little past the school and saw a bunch of boys playing baseball. We stood on the sidelines and watched for a while. Nobody had gloves or hats or helmets. The make-shift bases were pieces of tarpaper and the score was written in the dirt with a stick. But they had a bat and they had a ball and they were playing America's favorite pastime.

"We want to play," I said. "I'll go in the field and Miko can go with the side who's batting. That should even things out. Okay?" There was silence. Nobody made a peep, not even Miko. "Cat's got your tongue?" I said to no one and everyone at the same time.

"Veronica," Miko whispered. "Girls don't play baseball."

"What do you mean girls don't play baseball? Of course they do. I do! And actually, during

World War II they started the first professional women's league since all the men were fighting in the war." I stopped there and didn't continue. I guess I did know some history. Sports history, but it still was history and related to the war.

"Come on. Pitch the ball, Woody," yelled the batter. "Let's play."

"We want to play, too," I said again. "Why can't we play?"

"Because you're a girl and girls don't know how to play," said the catcher.

"Girls can't hit a ball," yelled someone from the outfield.

"I can outhit any one of you," I said. "Just give me a chance." There were giggles and laughs and general rudeness from the boys. And then Woody said, "Let her try."

The kid who was batting shoved the bat at me. I went up to the plate and dug my feet in the dirt. I spit in my hands and rubbed them together. Then I made the Sign of the Cross like the baseball players do on TV. I'm not Catholic, but I thought that would intimidate them.

"Give me your best stuff, Woody," I yelled.

"Don't worry about that," he shouted back. "I will."

I had been playing softball since I was seven so I felt pretty confident up there. Woody threw the first pitch with speed that would have made the Atlanta Braves proud. I swung and didn't even come close to the ball. "Had enough?" he yelled. I shook my head.

He slowed the next pitch down, but it sank so low that I couldn't reach it. "Are you finished yet, Miss Lady Baseball Player?"

"Not yet," I shot back.

"Keep your eye on the ball," Dad always yelled out to me. "Veronica, keep your eye on the ball." I felt Dad with me. I could almost hear him.

I connected with Woody's third pitch and watched it fly over the head of the center fielder. "Lucky shot," he called to me. The fourth was a solid shot past the third baseman. And the next pitch was a line drive up the middle that almost knocked Woody down.

"I didn't mean to do that," I called to him.

"Nice hitting, Miss Lady Baseball Player. You're on my team and so is Miko."

## 35

## It's Home

After the game, Miko walked me to Mrs. Matsui's place. I saw hundreds of buildings at Manzanar. They were all identical. They were made of wood and tarpaper and were lined in neat rows with fourteen barracks in each block. In addition, each grouping of buildings had a men's latrine and shower, women's latrine and shower, laundry and ironing room, mess hall, and a rec room.

Miko brought me to Mrs. Matsui's. She greeted us at the door and hugged each of us. "Thank you for bringing Veronica home, Miko. I hope you two had fun."

"We did," we said and giggled.

"From the giggling, it's best I not ask you what you were up to," she said. We giggled some more. "I'm glad you're such good friends," she added.

"Well, I have to go now," said Miko. "I don't want to worry Mama and Papa. See you tomorrow at school."

"Don't forget your poem," Mrs. Matsui reminded her.

"I already know it, Mrs. Matsui. Don't worry."

Mrs. Matsui lived in a single room with her husband and three children. The room was small, maybe twenty by twenty-five feet. It was very sparsely furnished—a table, a few chairs, some primitive shelving. I didn't see any beds. "My husband's quite the carpenter," she said as she caressed the table. "Don't you agree?"

"Yes, Ma'am," I answered.

"And my wife's the best seamstress in Manzanar," a man's voice added. I looked over and assumed the voice came from Mr. Matsui. "I didn't see you over there in the corner, Mr. Matsui. Hello. And yes, I agree. The curtains are beautiful."

"Let's go over to the mess hall now, Veronica," said Mrs. Matsui. "The boys are going to meet us over there for dinner. They've been outside all afternoon playing baseball." I smiled.

As we were leaving, I noticed a photograph of a woman on the table. It could have been Ms. Baumfree's twin. The face was identical but the hair and the dress and the period were all wrong. "Who's that lady?" I asked Mrs. Matsui.

"She's my good friend Izzy, Veronica. She's a friend in Los Angeles and she greatly helped our family. She's watching over all our belongings until we return. I don't know what we would have done without her."

We left the Matsui's room and went out to the mess hall. There were tables of people eating dinner. It seemed like the school cafeteria. Everything was served family-style and looked delicious. There was fried tofu, baked chicken, a medley of vegetables, and apple pie. Everyone except me piled their plates high with food. "You didn't put much on your plate," said Mr. Matsui. "Aren't you hungry, Veronica?"

"No, Mr. Matsui. I'm really not. I have a lot of homework to do and I want to get started before it gets too late."

"I think I should talk to that teacher of yours," he said and smiled at his wife.

"Do you think I can go over to the rec room to work on my poem after I eat, Mrs. Matsui?" I asked.

"It gets a little noisy there," she warned.

"I'll find a nice, quiet spot in a corner," I said. "The poem I'm reciting tomorrow is quite long and my memory isn't the greatest. I'll need some time to memorize it."

"All right, Veronica. Finish eating and then you may go. Be back by 8:00."

"Yes, Ma'am," I answered and then uncrossed my fingers.

When I got to the rec room, I saw some women sewing in the corner. I was very relieved. I went up to them and asked respectfully, "Could you please help me with something because I'm really not very good at sewing?" I took out the sheet with the purple flowers that I had tucked under my shirt. We only had two hours.

# 36

## Poetry for the Soul

I had a very restless night and was glad when morning arrived. My body hurt from sleeping on the floor, but I dare not complain. Everyone slept on the floor. Every night. We dressed for breakfast. "Mrs. Matsui, I'm not hungry and I still have a little work on my poem. May I skip breakfast and go right to the classroom and work there?"

"I hate for you to miss breakfast, Veronica, especially since you didn't eat much for dinner last night." She thought for a moment and said, "Go ahead. Take this apple and slice of bread and eat it on the way. I know you want to be prepared for our very special poetry sharing today."

"Thank you, Ma'am," I said.

I left our barracks and headed for school. I hadn't noticed the sentry yesterday in all the excitement of my first day at Manzanar—if it were my first day at Manzanar. The towers were tall. I could see armed soldiers pacing the catwalk up there. And barbed wire encircled the camp. "Are we that dangerous?" I thought. "I'm only eleven and the closest thing I have to a weapon is my pencil. Why are they so afraid of me?"

When I got to the classroom I took out the sheet and held it up to the wall. There only a few adjustments to make and I had about 45 minutes. I took out my needle and thread and started to work.

I took the last stitch as Miko walked in. I quickly put the needle and thread in my pocket. "What are you doing, Veronica?"

"Just practicing my poem," I said.

"It should be dramatic with all those purple flowers," she said. I didn't respond and stuck the sheet under my shirt.

Mrs. Matsui entered, followed by the rest of the children. They took their seats and she began. "Good morning, children."

"Good morning, Mrs. Matsui," they echoed in reply.

"I have been looking forward to today since the day we started our poetry unit. I know that you have been working very hard. I can't wait to hear your work. Poetry is a beautiful means of expression and I know you have a lot to say. You always do." She smiled.

"Kimii, would you start it for us?" Mrs. Matsu asked.

"I'd be honored," Kimii said as she got up and walked to the front of the room. She took a deep breath and began.

### Be Like the Cactus

*Let not harsh tongues, that wag in vain,*
*Discourage you. In spite of pain,*
*Be like the cactus, which through rain,*
*And storm, and thunder, can remain.*

164

Everyone applauded and Kimii sat down. I was in shock. I had never heard words put together with such meaning. I caught her eye and whispered, "That's beautiful, Kimii. That's really beautiful."

"Instead of calling you by name to recite," said Mrs. Matsui, "I'm going to ask you to approach the front of the room to share your poem as you feel the need."

Mary and Jessica got up together. They walked to the front of the room holding hands. Jessica went first.

### The World

*Who dares to say the world is filled*
*With putrid smells of hell to come,*
*The world shall hate, shall crush, ---*
*We live, we die, and all is done?*

*The Light of the World shall never cease*
*To those with heart and will;*
*The Life of Love will give us peace*
*At last when all is still.*

When Jessica was done, she moved aside and Mary recited.

### My Plea

*Oh God, I pray that I may bear a cross*
*To set my people free,*
*That I may help to take good-will across*
*An understanding sea.*

*Oh, God, I pray that someday every race*
*May stand on equal plane*
*And prejudice will find no dwelling place*
*In a peace that all may gain.*

I sat immobilized. I could not clap. I could not cheer. All I could do was wipe away my tears. I wasn't embarrassed because I saw that Mrs. Matsui had tears in her eyes, too. I sat there and listened to all my classmates. And then only Yukio and I were left. I didn't want to go, but Yukio took my hand and we walked up together. She went first.

*Faith*

> *My heart is proud,*
> *My soul is glorious and free.*
> *You, young Nisei, are fighting for*
> *our lives, our country, future,*
> *and everything we stand for.*

> *We are right behind you.*
> *You are proving that we are loyal*
> *in Italy and wherever you go.*
> *You will come back victorious and free,*
> *and we will be waiting for you*
> *in this land of liberty.*

It was finally my turn. I felt that my poem wasn't good enough to share. It wasn't long enough. It didn't have the emotion and the soul of the others. I stood there silent. Mrs. Matsui looked at me and nodded. I took a deep breath and cleared my throat. I couldn't disappoint her. I began.

> *Umbrella dogwood*
> *Filtering all life's evils*
> *Growls at my enemies*

When I finished, Yukio and I went to our places and sat down. The class was still applauding. Whether a

166

dream or not, I felt a part of my new family. "How appropriate to end with a haiku," said Mrs. Matsui. "It's the poetry of our people." I smiled and felt I belonged.

"You have all surpassed my expectations," said Mrs. Matsui. "You have bared your souls. I am so proud of you. Your poems will immortalize our time here. You have used your pens like swords."

"Cool," said Woody and we all laughed. We needed to laugh after that very heavy session. "Let's take a nice long recess," said Mrs. Matsui after that. "I think we all deserve one."

The children filed out, but I stayed behind and approached Mrs. Matsui. "I made something for you, for the class," I said. I pulled the sheet with the purple flowers from my shirt and handed it to her.

She opened up the bundle. "What's this, Veronica? The flowers are beautiful."

"They're curtains, Mrs. Matsui. I made us curtains," I said.

"They're lovely, Veronica. The colors are bold and I can almost smell the flowers. But our classroom doesn't have a window."

"I know that, Mrs. Matsui, but we can make a window with our curtains. There's a lot out there for us to see. We can see the world as we want to see it, not as we've been told."

# Epilogue

I can't forget the children I left. I can only hope they prospered. But that was not my choice. I was chosen for another mission, another life. My job was simple. Who chose me? Who gave me this gift? I don't know. All I know is that somehow, some way, I can travel through time, helping children.

Were these children so different from the ones I nurtured back in New York City in 1843? I don't think so. I feel, I believe, I was put on this earth to guide children to open doors so they can find their way. I take my children on a sojourn, a temporary trip, and I can only hope its effect will be permanent. My journey had brought me to the truth.

I received my gift the day I changed my name and started my life's mission. At Sojourner Truth Elementary I found myself 168 years into the future. I took its fifth graders on a trip. No, I guided them to the open door so they could take the journey themselves. It was always their choice. They could learn from their experiences or dismiss it as a dream. I hoped they would see history through the eyes of those who made history.

When each fifth grader came back from their sojourn, none talked about their travels. But I saw it in their eyes. I saw it in their attitudes. They changed and appreciated the world around them. They became kinder. They grew up.

Had I achieved my mission? I arrived in the classroom early that final morning waiting for the children to file in.

"Good morning," I said as they sat in my room for the last time.

"Good morning, Ms. Baumfree."

"I know that everyone connected with Sojourner Truth Elementary School expected me to revolutionize the social studies program this year. I didn't see that as my mission. My goal was to revolutionize each of you from within. I know a change has happened. I saw it when each of you returned. I watch it every day."

"What's she talking about?" Thomas asked with eyes downward.

"She's talking about our trips, Thomas, and you know it," said Veronica. "We're all just afraid to admit it. Afraid to be thought of as weird."

"A few of us girls talked and we all time-traveled," said Ellie. "We traveled and we met incredible people and did incredible things." Before Ellie could say another word, the class exploded. Everyone was talking at the same time, comparing experiences, sharing their feelings.

"Come on! They were just dreams," said Eric. "I thought it was real for a while, but the incandescent bulb didn't make it back."

"What do you mean?" said Ellie.

"I took one of Edison's light bulbs from his lab in Menlo Park. It was going to be my proof to myself that I was really there. No bulb returned with me. It was just an amazing dream."

"He's right," said David. "I stole the harmonica I was playing at Gettysburg. When I returned, I checked my pocket, praying it would be there. It wasn't."

I let the children talk for a short while and then rang my bell. "It's time to take off your watches," I said. "You don't need them any more."

"I really want to keep mine, Ms. Baumfree," said Gregory. "I want to travel again. I want to relive the past, even if it's just a dream."

"I need your watch, Gregory. Take them off please, children." The children took off their watches and I collected them. I put them in a very old satchel that I'd had for many, many years and closed it. "What are you going to do with them, Ms. Baumfree?" they asked.

I paused and then opened the satchel. I threw its contents on the table. "You're better than David Copperfield," said Shandra. "They're not wristwatches anymore."

"No, they're not. I've brought in a few artifacts for us to look at," I said. "I thought it would be a good way to review our year."

On the table lay a program from Ford's Theater dated April 14, 1865, a ship's manifest, a tiny parachute, a needle and thread, a copy of FDR's Thanksgiving Day speech, an old harmonica, a slice of Black Jack gum, and many other items.

Nobody said a word. They just smiled. The silence said it all.

I gave them a few more minutes. The bell was about to ring and our time together would be over. "You can travel whenever you like, children. You can travel with this," I said and placed their social studies book with the artifacts. "Knowing the past will help you write your futures, your stories, your history."

"Thanks Ms. Baumfree," said Gregory. "I hope you send my brother on a great trip next year."

"I won't be back next year. I have other work to do."

"What will Sojourner Truth do without you, Ms. Baumfree?" said Ellie.

"Sojourner and I are one and the same. When you get the chance, look us up."

# Historical Background

Ellie, Thomas, Vincent, Gregory, and Veronica are fictional characters. Most of the characters with whom they interact are also fictional. The time periods they explore are historically accurate as are the historical characters that are introduced.

In the case of our five main characters and all other characters, I have taken complete liberties, creating imaginary dialogue, actions, and circumstances.

# Prologue/Epilogue

## Sojourner Truth

Sojourner Truth was born into slavery in 1797 in Upstate New York. Her given name was Isabella Baumfree. She was first sold when she was nine years old. She had several owners and survived injustice and cruelty. New York outlawed slavery in 1827.

Isabella settled in New York City and on June 1, 1843, she changed her name to Sojourner Truth. She had a religious experience telling her to travel (sojourn) and seek the truth. She became a preacher, speaking out against slavery. She championed women's rights and other causes to seek justice for all people.

# Ellie's Story

## Warm Springs, Georgia

At the turn of the twentieth century Warm Springs became a popular vacation resort for the wealthy. The spa boasted buoyant, 88 degree waters year-round. Well-to-do families from the area built summer homes and the Meriwether Inn, a 118-room facility, opened on a hill overlooking the springs.

President Roosevelt visited Warm Springs at the request of George Foster Peabody, a wealthy banker and personal friend. Peabody told Roosevelt of substantial improvement another victim of polio had experienced at the springs. Roosevelt visited Warm Springs and the waters gave him relief and seemed to improve his weakened muscles.

Roosevelt used two-thirds of his personal wealth to purchase the Inn, the springs, and 1,200 acres in 1926. He established the Georgia Warm Springs Foundation on July 28, 1927. He visited Warm Springs 41 times. On April 12, 1945, President Roosevelt died at the Little White House, his home in Warm Springs.

## President Franklin D. Roosevelt

Franklin Roosevelt was the 32$^{nd}$ President of the United States (1933-1945). In 1921 he was stricken with polio. He purchased a resort at Warm Springs, Georgia, in 1926, where he founded a hydrotherapy center for the treatment of polio patients.

**Eleanor Roosevelt**

Eleanor Roosevelt was married to Franklin Roosevelt. The First Lady visited Warm Springs several times.

**Suzanne Pike**

Suzanne, nicknamed "Suzie" by President Roosevelt, was a patient at Warm Springs. She met President Roosevelt when she was very young and spent many years at Warm Springs in his company. I am proud to say she is my friend.

**Mrs. Huntington**

Mrs. Huntington was a teacher at Warm Springs.

**Fala**

Fala was President Roosevelt's black Scottish terrier. Fala was born on April 7, 1940, so wouldn't have been with President Roosevelt in 1933 when Ellie visits Warm Springs. I took the liberty of rearranging time so Fala could be a part of Ellie's story.

## Thomas' Story

**The Berlin Airlift**

After World War II, Germany was divided into four sectors. The Allies—the United States, France, Great

Britain, and the Soviet Union—each patrolled one sector respectively. The Soviets occupied the eastern half while the Americans, British and French occupied the western half.

That worked for a few years but then the Soviet Union had major disagreements with the other three countries about how to govern. The Soviets were against capitalism and democracy and believed in a communist state. They ruled their section that way. The problem was that the capital city of Berlin was totally in the Soviets' sector. The Americans, British, and French had been bringing food and supplies to the Germans in West Berlin. But then the Soviets sealed off Berlin from the Americans, British, and French. They wouldn't allow trains and trucks to bring in supplies. West Berliners were in danger of starving.

The Soviets said that they would gladly feed the Germans in the Allied sections of West Berlin but they would have to adhere to Communist principles. Most Germans refused and said they would rather starve to death than give up their freedom. The Allies decided to airlift food and supplies.

### Lt. Gail Halvorsen

Lt. Halvorsen was an American pilot who airlifted supplies to West Berlin during the Berlin Airlift. It was his idea to drop chocolate and gum to the children of Berlin, earning him the nickname "Onkel Wackel-flügel."

## Peter

Peter Zimmerman was a child in Berlin who wrote to Onkel Wackelflügel requesting candy. He did receive a package.

## Mercedes

Mercedes Simon did have white chickens in her yard which failed to produce eggs due to the planes flying nonstop overhead. She wrote Onkel Wackelflügel and received chocolate.

## Vincent's Story

## Ellis Island

The federal immigration station at Ellis Island opened January 1, 1892. It closed in 1954. During that period, over 12 million immigrants were processed by the U. S. Bureau of Immigration. Industrialization in the United States drew eager workers from dozens of foreign nations. More than one million people came through its doors in 1907, the peak year of immigration. April 17, 1907 was the largest single day with 11,747 immigrants processed.

Immigrants spent two to five hours during processing. Arrivals were asked 29 questions including name, occupation, and background questions. Those with visible health problems were either sent home or held in the island's hospital facilities. About 2 percent were sent back to their mother countries for disease, criminal records, or insanity. To them Ellis Island became known as "The Island of Tears" or "Heartbreak Island." The Kissing Post was a wooden column outside the Registry Room where new arrivals would meet their relatives and friends, usually with hugs and kisses.

## Gregory's Story

### The Children's March on Birmingham

Between 1957 and 1963 there were 18 bombings in Birmingham, Alabama. There were no arrests. Blacks were attacked. There were no arrests. Freedom Riders were almost beaten to death in 1961. There were no arrests.

Dr. Martin Luther King, Jr. tried to draw attention to the terrible problems in Birmingham but he couldn't do it alone. Black adults were afraid to march. They were afraid to lose their jobs. They were afraid that matters would get worse.

The children of Birmingham were afraid, too. But they were more afraid of what would happen if they didn't let the world know of the problems in Birmingham. They marched. They marched and were arrested. They were arrested and woke up a race-divided America to the horrors happening in Birmingham.

## Dr. Martin Luther King, Jr.

Dr. King was a clergyman and a civil rights leader who believed in non-violence.

## Rev. Fred Shuttlesworth

Rev. Shuttlesworth was a civil rights activist and minister in Birmingham, Alabama. He co-founded the Southern Christian Leadership Conference.

## Shelley "The Playboy" Stewart

Shelley Stewart was a DJ at WENN in Birmingham, Alabama. He was known as "The Mouth of the South."

## Rev. James Bevel

Rev. Bevel was a civil rights activist and a top lieutenant of the Rev. Martin Luther King.

## Eugene "Bull" Connor

Bull Connor was the Commissioner of Public Safety in Birmingham in 1963.

## John F. Kennedy

John F. Kennedy was the 35th President of the United States (1961-1963). His initiative for civil rights legislation led to the Civil Rights Act of 1964.

## John-John Kennedy

John F. Kennedy, Jr. was President Kennedy's son. He was born Nov. 25, 1960.

## Veronica's Story

## Manzanar

Manzanar was one of ten Japanese relocation camps established after the bombing of Pearl Harbor. President Franklin D. Roosevelt issued Executive Order 9066 which permitted the military to round-up and incarcerate approximately 120,000 persons of Japanese ancestry who were living on the West Coast. Most were U. S. citizens or legal permanent resident aliens. Half were children.

These Japanese-Americans were forced to leave their homes and leave their jobs. Sometimes family members were put in different camps. They were incarcerated for up to four years without any legal recourse. Some died due to extreme emotional stress and inadequate medical care.

During World War II, Executive Order 9066 was justified as a "military necessity" to protect the United States against spying and sabotage. It was later documented that there had not been one instance of disloyalty by any Japanese-American.

Almost 50 years later, Congress passed the Civil Liberties Act of 1988. Better known as the Japanese American Redress Bill, this act acknowledged that a "grave injustice was done" and mandated that

Congress pay each victim of internment $20,000 in reparations.

## The Poems

The poems shared by the children during the poetry recitation were written by children in Manzanar. Veronica's haiku was not.

# Bibliography

Cherny, Andrei. *The Candy Bomber: The Untold Story of the Berlin Airlift and America's Finest Hour.* New York: Berkley Caliber, 2008.

Cooper, Michael L. *Fighting for Honor: Japanese Americans and World War II.* New York: Clarion Books, 2000.

Cooper, Michael L. *Remembering Manzanar: Life in a Japanese Relocation Camp.* New York: Clarion Books, 2002.

Dunn, Marion. Personal interview. 5 September 2010.

"Ellis Island." History.com. 1996-2011. A&E Television Networks. 17 Jan. 2011. <http://www.history.com/topics/ellis-island>.

Elmer, Robert. *Candy Bombers.* Grand Rapids: zonderkidz, 2006.

Friedler, Sorelle. "World War II Poetry: A Paper Comparing World War II Poetry." <http//www.sccs.swarthmore.edu/users/04/sorelle/poetry/wwii/paper.html>.

Halvorsen, Gail S. *The Berlin Candy Bomber.* Bountiful: Horizon Publishers, 1997.

"Internment History: Children of the Camps." PBS. 1999. <http://www.pbs.org/childofcamps/history/index.html>.

*Mighty Times: The Children's March.* Directors Robert Hudson and Bobby Houston. Teaching Tolerance in association with Home Box Office, Inc., 2005.

Pike, Suzanne. Personal interview. 22 February 2011.

"Ramstein Air Base." U. S. Air Force. 12 Jan. 2011. <http://www.ramstein.af.mil>.

Raven, Margot Theis. *Mercedes and the Chocolate Pilot.* Chelsea: Sleeping Bear Press, 2002.

Reeves, Pamela. *Ellis Island: Gateway to the American Dream.* New York: Barnes & Noble Books, 1998.

Roosevelt, Franklin D. Presidential Address. Thanksgiving Day. Warm Springs, Georgia. 30 Nov. 1933.

Sapp, Jeff. *Mighty Times: The Children's March.* Montgomery: Teaching Tolerance, 2005.

Stanley, Jerry. *I am an American: A True Story of Japanese Internment.* New York: Crown Publishers, Inc., 1994.

Tunnell, Michael O. *Candy Bomber: The Story of the Berlin Airlift's "Chocolate Pilot".* Watertown: Charlesbridge, 2010.

*Warm Springs.* Director Joseph Sargent. HBO Films, Home Box Office, Inc., 2005.

Warm Springs Historic Site Tour. Warm Springs, Georgia. 6 Apr. 2010.

Welch, Gwendolyn Guster. Personal interview. 26 January 2011.

Yancey, Diane. *Life in a Japanese American Internment Camp.* San Diego: Lucent Books, 1998.

# Thank You

Mike Shadix, librarian and archivist at the Roosevelt Warm Springs Institute for Rehabilitation, spent many hours helping me navigate through the Institute's archives. He was instrumental in locating information that made Ellie's story come alive with rich details and accuracy. Thank you, Mike.

Linda Creekbaum, docent and tour guide at the Institute, spent an afternoon taking me around the buildings and grounds of the Institute. Her knowledge of the Roosevelt years and her passion for this period were inspirational. Thank you, Linda.

Robin Glass, Roosevelt's Little White House site manager, escorted me around the museum and pointed out important information. He graciously answered the many questions that I had. Thank you, Robin.

Marion Dunn, pushboy during the Roosevelt years, helped this period come alive for me. He shared many stories while we were gathered at the pools. Marion has an incredible memory and sure knows how to tell a story. Thank you, Marion.

And now for Suzanne... Where do I start? I met Suzanne about ten years ago when I visited Warm Springs with my fifth grade class. She mesmerized us with stories of her times at the Institute with President Roosevelt...with Rosie. She made history come alive for us year after year as I returned with other classes.

When I retired from teaching and finally had the time to write the Warm Springs story, I came to

Suzanne for help. She shared her memories with me as we dined in Georgia Hall, the place where Roosevelt hosted his Thanksgiving Dinners. She is the soul, the inspiration, the heart of the Warm Springs episode with Ellie. Thank you, Suzanne. I love you.

Gwendolyn Guster Welch was very gracious in supplying me with the names of the different schools that Negroes attended in Birmingham in 1963. Thank you, Gwendolyn.

Connie Accardi Lynam, my best friend since fourth grade, was born in Palermo, Italy. Her family came to the United States when she was a young girl. Her Italian heritage and strong family bonds served as an inspiration for Vincent's story. Thank you, Concetta.

Rhodes and Paul White and Kathy Scheer read early drafts of *Social Studies Makes Me Sleepy* and gave me invaluable feedback. Thank you, Rhodes, Paul, and Kathy.

Karen Huban helped proof and edit *Social Studies Makes Me Sleepy*. Her keen eye and meticulous nature go unparalleled. Thank you, Karen.

Michele Phillips is my artistic angel. Her talent, her passion, her research for historical accuracy and detail brought *Social Studies Makes Me Sleepy* to life as nobody else could. Thank you, Michele.

Ahmad Meradji and Omid Meradji with BookLogix Publishing Services have guided me and held my hand along the way. They literally put this book together. Thank you, Ahmad and Omid.

Last, but not least. Thank you, John, for everything. You are the best writer I know and your mastery of the written word inspires me. You have helped me in every facet of this book and I couldn't have done it without you.